# OFF THE FRAME

## The Lighter Side of Tennis

ALISTAIR HIGHAM & RONALD CARTER

ILLUSTRATIONS BY DAVE SLANEY

# ABOUT THE AUTHORS

**Ronald Carter** is a professor of English at the University of Nottingham, UK. He knows a bit about watching tennis but a bit more about writing. He was awarded an MBE in 2009 for services to higher education but has no awards whatsoever for anything to do with any sport.

**Alistair Higham** has played and coached at all levels from club to international and has held roles such as LTA Head of Coach Development, 16U GB National Coach and Tennis Foundation Universities Manager. He has also written extensively about matchplay momentum. To find out more, visit www.momentuminsport.com

**Dave Slaney** knows absolutely nothing about tennis, but a bit about drawing. He hasn't played tennis at any level, apart from at school and rackets were wooden. He teaches Karate which Ron and Alistair thought might be useful.

# OFF THE FRAME

L.S. T.C.

LONG SHOTT TENNIS CLUB
*Since 1876*

ENTHUSIASTICUS
DESPITUS
ELEMENTUM

## The Lighter Side of Tennis

ALISTAIR HIGHAM & RONALD CARTER

Typeset in Garamond 11pt.
by Freestyle
3 Pelham Road
Nottingham
NG5 1AP
www.freestyleuk.com

ISBN 978-0-9574652-0-6

YOU'LL DISCOVER WHEN YOU ARRIVE,
THE JOURNEY IS THE PRIZE

Mike Scott

# FOREWORD

*Off The Frame: Tennis Tales from Bogshire* was first published in 1997. Over the years many people have told us how much they have enjoyed the stories. Why, therefore, embark upon an updated edition with new additions and cartoons? Why make changes?

First of all, many of the most popular stories have been retained, although they have been re-moulded to bring them up-to-date and to reflect the new setting of Long Shott Tennis Club in Spin Valley. But, most importantly, we felt we wanted to add new stories that reflected some of the major changes in the fabric of everyday life over the past fifteen years since *Off The Frame* was first published. They reflect changes in the ways in which we communicate with an increased use of the internet for purposes of contact, coaching and everyday communication; they reflect a habitual use of websites for information and networking and they reflect the ways in which the world has simultaneously become a smaller place.

The new stories have a more international appeal as, even though they are still rooted in the experience of the authors in playing, coaching and watching tennis (despite the rain) in British clubs, they have also become more outward-looking. Indeed, one of our new stories features a cast-list of international players and coaches.

The book also reflects changes in publishing that have altered our practices of book buying, listening and viewing as well as some fundamental shifts in reading habits. Yes, books are still read by turning paper pages but increasingly we are reading e-books and listening to audiobooks, we are watching author interviews on *YouTube* and we are downloading and experiencing tracks of poetry played to words and music. We wanted to ensure that *Off The Frame* embraced these changes and became much more something that we could also read and experience through a variety of different media.

Plans for future developments of *Off The Frame* will continue to evolve and will embrace many of these multi-media developments. But a book is still a book and we hope that this book will continue to underline the contrasts between the serious and the less serious, the higher and lower reaches of the game and the ups and downs of basic human emotions that all in their different ways make up, as our new subtitle now has it,
*'The Lighter Side of Tennis'.*

Alistair Higham and Ronald Carter.
Nottingham 2012.

# ACKNOWLEDGEMENTS

Many friends and colleagues too numerous to mention have played a part in the interweaving of imaginative truths and fictions which form the basis for *Off The Frame*.

However, the authors wish to thank, in particular, the following for having in various ways provided us with specific support, encouragement and in some cases critical comments on the material for this book as it has developed from a rich variety of anecdotes, discussions and personal experiences: Cassie Bradley; Jane Carter; Mark Cox; Paul Dent; Joanne Higham; Andy Higham; Jonny Higham; Liz Jones; Darren Kirk; Tim Phillips; Keith Reynolds; Jenny Thomas; Ben Price; Mike Robinson; Jesse Rowe; Mike Scott; Dave Slaney; Cheralynne Todd; Carlos Vicens; Martin Weston.

Special thanks go Martin Weston whose artistic interpretation set the original tone for the cartoons in *Off The Frame*. They still make us laugh and several of the illustrations in this book are true to Martin's original ideas.

# LIST OF MAIN CHARACTERS

| | |
|---|---|
| 'Rocket' Eastwood | A player with canon-ball power (but no backhand) |
| Mitch Robinson | The club captain and tennis 'Trickster' |
| Cedric Ballsworthy | A humane, partially-sighted umpire |
| Arkwright Stone | A tennis farmer who digs deep |
| Clegg Stone | Son of Arkwright |
| Jeff Ghandi | The vegetarian club coach |
| Lurch McFly Sharkey McFly | A dangerous doubles team |
| Mrs Slade-Lipkin | Ball-girl trainer extraordinaire |
| Charles de Beauvoir | Golden Mr Glorious |
| Bill McNab | An on-court huffer and puffer |
| Oliver Mottershed | A referee; an officious official |
| Alison Scott | Computer whizz and tennis 'improver' |
| Carlos Soltana | The Spanish Coach |
| Destini Dream | An American teenage tennis sensation |
| Robert Speed | A reluctant e-coach |
| Mrs Barbara Tiffin | An anxious tennis parent |
| Katie Robinson | Tennis Agony Aunt |

# STORIES & POEMS

1.    Mitch: Long Shott Men's Team Captain

2.    The Trickster

3.    Rocket Shot

4.    E-Coach

5.    Home Advantage

6.    The Court

7.    Long Shott Tennis Club's Grass Court Championships

8.    Overheads To Pay

9.    Another Lob

10.   Jeff (Long Shott's spiritual Head Coach)
      v. Arkwright (The Tennis Farmer)

11.   Lessons Of Tennis

12.   Spin Valley International

13.   Mitch Match

14.   It's Good To Talk

15.   Racket Rocket Science

16.   Parents Under Surveillance

17.   Dear Mixed Troubles

18.   Calling The Shots

19.   A Rush Of Air

20.   The Spin Valley Tennis Glossary

# 'MITCH'

## LONG SHOTT MEN'S TEAM CAPTAIN

*Mitch is Long Shott's Men's Team Captain. He is well liked on account of his sense of fair play, his sense of humour and his relaxed attitude to mechanical problems with his cars. Mitch's attempt to win a record tenth Long Shott Club Open Championships rests on the outcome of a seemingly unrelated match during which a devious plan is formed by some of his friends.*

Mitch was a very popular character at Long Shott Tennis Club and throughout Spin Valley. He had played in the Men's first team for twenty six years in a row and he had been captain for the past ten years.

His popularity was due to a number of reasons. Firstly, he was fair. So fair, in fact, that his fairness would often mentally destroy players who cheated. At the first opportunity of confrontation they would come forward angrily demanding "Are you telling me that shot was out?" "No," replied Mitch cheerfully. "Great shot, just caught the line." After that the wind had gone out of their confrontationally competitive sails.

Secondly, he was naturally skillful. He played with great accuracy, a deceptive change of pace and a detailed knowledge of a wide range of wrong footing shots. Known on court as 'The Trickster', he had inspired the new generation of players in Spin Valley, several of whom hit perfect low to high backhands. One of them (who went on to play outside Spin Valley), as a twelve year old was so impressed with Mitch playing a winning backhand smash in an exhibition match that he asked for his autograph. He still has the autograph book though he has yet to see Mitch hit another winning backhand smash.

1

Thirdly, he had a sense of humour on court. Like many tennis players he used the word "Long", if a shot landed just beyond the line. But when Mitch hit a weak lob, as his partner dived for cover and the opposition moved forward to bury the smash, he would often loudly announce "Short."

Finally, Mitch is prone to bad fortune with cars. As a result, he has achieved in Spin Valley a legendary, almost mythical status with his car stories. Indeed, it would be difficult to drop Mitch from the club side as team spirit would undoubtedly suffer if the transport was too straight forward. The disasters are always accompanied by the kind of good luck you sense he may always have. His work van once exploded into flames just as he had got out and was walking away from it. When a screeching noise developed from his front left wheel one week while he was transporting players to and from the hotel at a tournament in the far south, he stopped every fifteen minutes and disappeared underneath it with a small can of '3-in-1 oil' designed for bicycle chains. Two weeks later on a deserted country lane in Spin Valley, the front wheel of his car fell off and careered down the road in front of him. He later reported that he felt a bump, saw a wheel rolling and said to himself "That's my wheel!" Typically, the next car coming down the road was a friend of his doubles partner Rocket, heading to Clopton on business.

On one occasion, he overloaded his joiner's van with so much wood that it seemed dangerous to a police officer following behind him. The police car pursued him down the lane to his house, flashing him to pull over. When Mitch finally stopped on the far side of his yard, the police car pulled up behind him. The

2

young officer got out, only to watch in horror as Mitch reversed into his panda car, carefully depositing onto it the full weight of wood as he did so. Mitch got out and said "Sorry Officer. Didn't see you there. I think I had too much wood loaded on." Being at the time on private land, Mitch avoided prosecution.

Due to all of the above, Mitch was popular and inspired great loyalty. It was because of this popularity that, when he was due to withdraw through illness one year in the Long Shott Tennis Club Open Championships, a plan was formed by his team mates to help him out.

Mitch had made it through to the third round of the singles but on the evening he was due to play, was suffering from a migraine. He reckoned he would be better the next day and, with his opponent's consent, had requested that the match be postponed. Kindly local referee, Cedric Ballsworthy would certainly have agreed to this but he was on holiday and the officious replacement, Mr Oliver Mottershed, refused to allow it. As the day wore on and his match approached Mitch tried to sleep it off in his hotel room nearby. The talk amongst the other players was of the referee's unsympathetic decision which looked like ending Mitch's chances of taking the title a record tenth time.

As things went, the matches on the court where Mitch was due to play were very long. So long in fact, that when the match before Mitch's commenced there was obviously only a limited amount of daylight left. With this in mind, a further request was made to Mr Mottershed from Mitch's doubles partner, Rocket. Surely he could now be allowed an extra day - the tournament could not be advanced, even if Mitch went on, the match would certainly not be completed. Mr Mottershed, however, had an iron will when it came to flexibility.

"Certainly not. As Club Captain, he is surely familiar with Rule 2.5.5" said Mottershed.

Rocket stared at him and replied in a deadpan voice: "Now let's think. He certainly knows 2.5.4 and 2.5.6, he may even have a basic grasp of 2.5.7 but I'm not sure about 2.5.5."

This went completely over Mottershed's head and, as if having a normal conversation, he replied:

"Rule 2.5.5 clearly states that 'A competitor shall undertake to be available during all the published hours of play of the tournament, and at any other times within the published dates deemed necessary by the Referee to complete the tournament, unless written permission for absence is obtained from the referee in advance' and I'm afraid I have no official headed note paper with me at present."

"Git," murmured Rocket as he closed the door behind him.

As Rocket walked away from the referee's office, an announcement came over the tannoy:

"Would all competitors please ensure they are familiar with the conditions of entry. Thank you."

"Creep," murmured Rocket.

The match before the one which Mitch was due to play was now on court. It was being contested between Charles de Beauvoir and Bill McNab. Charles de Beauvoir was a new face in the tournament. He lived in the neighbouring, much richer region of Manorshire. Manorshire was a much stronger tennis region and de Beauvoir had come to Spin Valley pot hunting. He had always been less than gracious about Long Shott and so, unsurprisingly, was not too popular with the locals.

Now in his thirties, de Beauvoir had a fine physique, a golden tan and not a hair out of place. His tennis was every bit as fancy as his name and he treated it like an art. On court he was 'Mr Glorious': he could play reverse spin drop shots, cannonball forehands, deft lobs, backhand smashes; he could look one way and flick it the other. His only problem was that these shots didn't always go in.

McNab, on the other hand, was a roadrunner. He couldn't do anything but shovel his forehand, poke his backhand and run all day retrieving the ball. But he took his tennis very seriously and advised himself out loud between points.

Unfortunately for Mitch, who was feeling no better, the match was passing quickly. De Beauvoir was on form and was leading 5-0 in the first set. It was then that Rocket realised that if McNab could somehow make the match last longer, it may go dark before Mitch came on and therefore Mitch's match would have to be postponed. He had to get some support for McNab. Rocket went and assembled his team-mates and they started to clap and encourage McNab. Even though it was getting dark and cold, the motivation to stay and support was high - they could not miss the opportunity of helping Mitch, encouraging the opponent of Mr Glorious and outwitting Oliver Mottershed all in one go.

In addition, McNab's comments to himself were providing some amusement. Bill McNab was not a bright man and, when he spoke out loud, he did so in a deep, slow voice with a heavy accent. Furthermore, he spoke in a hesitant manner which suggested that he was still working out the sentences as he spoke them. He seemed completely unaware of any humour contained in what he was saying or in his unique style of delivery.

The small crowd became aware of his comments at the end of the first set when he said to himself, "Come on. You are playing just like......yourself." The next two points went by, largely unnoticed as everyone tried to get their head around that one, when, having just missed a passing shot  McNab said: "How many times do you have to be told? Just put your head down and bang it as hard as you can."

He was an instant hit with the crowd and they started to get behind him in a big way. Despite not having won a game in the first set, the strange tennis scoring system did as it always does and granted him the favour of 0-0 as the second set began.  This in itself can provide an excellent opportunity for the player who is losing.

McNab was aware of this and, in order to show how fit and ready he was for the beginning of the second set, he did a swift ten press ups as part of his return of serve routine.  His routine was enough to distract de Beauvoir into double faulting on the first point.  Two net cords and a missed smash later and to the delight of his supporters, McNab changed ends at 1-0 up.  De Beauvoir started to show the early signs of frustration.  He was annoyed that he had won six perfect games to his opponent's one lucky game and yet he was still losing this set.

His growing temper was not allayed when he looked up to see his opponent bouncing up and down, blowing air out loudly through his mouth as part of his new service routine.  Nor did he feel any calmer when McNab's first serve hit a stone, rolled for an ace and the crowd cheered. His frustration lead to errors and he hit two returns in the net and one out to go 2-0 down. He stood to serve and looked up.  McNab was jumping, spinning and blowing like a whirling dervish.  He fell into the trap and proceeded to try to hit the cover off the ball to teach his opponent a lesson. He served two first serves over the baseline, hit a forehand in the stop fence and a backhand in the bottom of the net to go 3-0 down. McNab ran proudly into the change of ends as if doing a lap of honour.

At that point normality returned and despite McNab retrieving some incredible shots, de Beauvoir had calmed down. He won the next three games as McNab reflected to himself: "You have just played eight of the world's shortest rallies." Quickly followed by "Nine."

The match was now level at 3-3. During this game at 30-30 they had another long rally which ended in McNab diving to scoop a backhand off his frame to go for a winner on the sharpest angle cross court. It had all the hallmarks of a double hit.

De Beauvoir came to the net and demanded in an indignant voice: "I say, did you hit that last shot twice?" McNab looked at his opponent and in an equally indignant voice said "Twice? I was lucky to hit the bugger once."

He returned to the baseline and started his energetic dancing. De Beauvoir just stood at the net. Rocket, recognising an excellent opportunity to waste a few more minutes, shouted across "Wait there, I'll get the referee" and went to the referee's office.

He went into the office and said innocently to Mottershed, "Sorry to bother you. Would you mind just reminding us what happens if a ball should strike a permanent fixture during a rally?"

Mottershed began: "Certainly. Firstly, let us be clear on what constitutes a permanent fixture....."

Five minutes later Rocket said "Thank you, that's most clear now. Oh, by the way, there is a dispute on court two and they have requested your assistance." Mottershed positively ran out of the office and arrived on court two to find de Beauvoir still standing at the net and McNab sweating profusely as he continued to dance on the baseline.

Despite all his knowledge the referee did as referees often do and said it was up to the player who hit it to call. McNab was not about to concede, at this point, that it was anything other than a clean hit and the game continued.

At this stage, the light was beginning to fade slightly. Greatly encouraged by the possibility of their plan working, the crowd renewed their support for their new hero, McNab. He was running from side to side, shovelling the ball back and blowing loudly for all he was worth. Rarely had this level of hacking been seen in Spin Valley as the ball came back time and time again. But de Beauvoir really had him on the end of a string, standing well inside the court now and totally in control of the rally, he played a dropshot followed by a lob. McNab set off after the lob and somehow got it back. De Beauvoir played an angled volley, which again was scraped back and now had an open court with the easiest of shots into a big gap.

However McNab was not giving up and on his last legs, he made one last effort to run towards the gap. As McNab staggered, off balance and gasping towards the open court, de Beauvoir, clearly enjoying having his opponent totally at his mercy, flicked it back behind him. McNab had no legs to turn again and could only watch in pain as he ran without choice away from the ball. His pain turned to joy as he saw the shot float beyond the line and bounce out. He yelled out: "Ha. Fooled him!" And then after a few seconds... "Completely!" The crowd clapped enthusiastically. He was now 5-3 up in the second set.

De Beauvoir, now looked like a man under pressure. It seemed as if his tan had faded, his gold chain had less sparkle, and some strands of hair had fallen out of place. He was further frustrated by the line call argument on the very next point; he called a ball out and McNab came forward to query the call. The frustration came not in the argument itself but in the way McNab kept repeating the question to end all questions:

"Yes I know it was out, but how far out....is out?" This phrase immediately entered the folklore of Spin Valley tennis and Spin Valley University philosophers have whiled away many an hour contemplating this very question.

Eventually, McNab accepted he had lost the point and carried on. Still bemused by the question, however, de Beauvoir lost the next two points. McNab was now just two points away from winning the set and the light was fading quickly.

The next rally was another long one. After twenty shots, de Beauvoir again played a dropshot. McNab slipped as he ran for it but managed to scoop it up only to fall to the ground by the net as the ball bounced up harmlessly just on the other side. Sitting now two inches away from the net, he watched through the strings as de Beauvoir came in for the kill from a bounce smash. In a desperate attempt to distract his opponent, McNab held his racket above the height of the net. Further incensed by this, de Beauvoir smashed the ball as hard as he could, from less than three feet away, straight at him. It hit McNab's outstretched racket and shot back for a clean winner. The crowd clapped and cheered wildly.

As far as de Beauvoir was concerned that was enough for one evening. In near pitch darkness, on set point to McNab, from his return, he smacked the ball right out of the ground and yelled: "Now get that back, you talentless hacker."

The match had to be postponed until the next day and the plan to help Mitch had succeeded.

The next day de Beauvoir phoned in sick and didn't turn up to finish the match. Nor, indeed, did he return for any future tournaments.

Mitch recovered to go on to win a record tenth title.

# THE 'TRICKSTER'

You might have seen him play before,
Though he's getting rare these days,
And though his shorts are back in style,
He's from a different age.

He's no respect for racket trends,
"It's just a modern con"
But no-one really listens,
They think he's nearly 'gone'.

With returns so weak and feeble,
His chances look remote,
But he'll dink it to you softly,
Then stuff it down your throat.

He'll wrap you on the wrong foot,
Turn you inside out,
Drop his shots precisely,
And listen, while you shout:

"I've never played this bad before!"
To those laughing at the side,
Unaware still at the rallies end,
You've been taken for a ride.

Because his craft is well concealed,
In a camouflaged disguise,
And when you're looking long and deep,
You'll find it short and wide.

"I'll give this crafty trickster,
A taste of modern stuff!"
But your semi-western passing shot's,
Not solved his double bluff.

You'll bob and weave, and duck and dive,
Yet he just seems to flow,
With lots of time to choose his shots,
While you're a yard too slow.

So you madly sprint across the court,
In a frenzied show of power,
While the ball just floats the other way,
At fourteen miles per hour.

"You jammy sod!" you cry out loud,
As his third lob hits the line,
But you're only sobbing quietly,
When he's done it twenty times.

And when the match is finished,
And you can't believe you lost,
You'll want to smash your rackets,
Not matter what they cost.

You'll not feel any better,
When you're told by a so-called mate,
That he hasn't had his racket strung,
Since nineteen eighty-eight.

# ROCKET SHOT

*Mitch isn't there when Rocket needs him. This leaves Rocket facing an uncomfortable decision in a crucial club league match. Will the Long Shott Tennis Club Men's Team avoid relegation?*

It was often rumoured that to get into the Long Shott Tennis Club Men's team you had to own a car and be prepared not to bill the club for petrol expenses. An even more certain bet was, however, to be able to hit a backhand with a half-decent low to high swing.

Rocket was a member of the Long Shott Tennis Club Men's team in Spin Valley. Rocket did not own a car and he didn't have a half-decent low to high swing on his backhand. Rocket didn't even have a swing on his backhand. In fact, his backhand rarely went anywhere at all, let alone with a recognisable swing.

Rocket was in the team for his serve and his forehand, both shots occasionally hit with such ferocity that in the bar after matches people would often say that he had once given lessons to the young Andy Roddick. Rocket was the mainstay of the Long Shott Tennis Club team and his power struck fear into opposing teams.

It was not altogether fair to say that Rocket could not play a backhand, although he did tend to describe it as "the other shot." His technique is best described as unorthodox, resembling the kind of reverse flick used for digging out soft-scoop ice-cream. When in contact with the ball (and complete misses were not infrequent) the action produced a floating, looping result which could bamboozle even the most experienced of opponents. However, for a player of his somewhat one-dimensional talents, the selection of an appropriate doubles partner would test even the most astute of captains.

But Long Shott had the solution in Mitch. Mitch complemented Rocket's skills. In contrast to Rocket's power, Mitch delicately played all soft spins and tricky angles and being a left-hander, was more comfortable in the backhand court. He also had the kind of pace around a court which could make up for any lethargic partner. This meant he would often cover for Rocket, a big man and not known for his deftness on the backhand side. "Mine" was a call often heard on the tennis courts at Long Shott. It was nearly always Mitch, shouting to remove Rocket from his path as he scampered, much to Rocket's relief, to play the forehand which had looked destined for Rocket's backhand soft scoop dig.

The Long Shott Tennis Club Men's Team enjoys the rare distinction of never having been relegated. The simple reason for this is that they are in the fifth of five divisions and can go no lower. The team rarely wins singles matches but they have enjoyed some fine doubles victories. Rocket and Mitch's doubles matches are nearly always close and none was closer than one crunch match against Midtown, one late July evening in the sleepy coastal resort that had been echoing all weekend with the team's shouts of "Mine." The local paper, much to Rocket's gratification, had run a back page headline on the prodigious power of the Long Shott Man's serve, reporting how Rocket had performed the hitherto unsurpassed feat of serving one ball from the tennis court into the clubhouse of the Bowls Club, landing a good 100 metres beyond the wire mesh marking the perimeter of the court.

On paper Midtown had the strongest team but the match was

played on grass not on paper. It was also played in tropical heat and humidity and both teams were battling to avoid the ignominy of being the bottom of league five; the team that would be relegated if only further relegation had been possible. The final match of the final doubles had reached a critical point: third set; 4 all; 30-40, break point with the opposition serving. As the teams were tied in all matches played so far, the whole Midtown match would hinge on the outcome and, ironically, on the way Rocket would face the challenge of playing the most crucial backhand of his tennis life.

At this stage in the match a small crowd, including the whole Long Shott team, had gathered and were already absorbed by the quality of the long rally played to decide this crucial breakpoint. Suddenly, one of the Midtown players, who were both by this time at the net, unexpectedly played a soft scoop dig of a backhand, causing the ball to float high in the air towards the tramlines on Rocket's side of the court and straight into the path of his backhand. Rocket moved towards the ball with a slightly knowing expression and even had time to look smugly at his opponents as he waited for Mitch's call, knowing that his partner would soon scamper round for the inevitable, even relatively simple, left-handed forehand kill.

Mitch's call of "Mine" however, failed to materialise and it slowly but surely dawned on Rocket that this was his shot. A cumbersome mover at his best, Rocket managed to register in his movements almost every available possibility for shot execution whilst his expression changed from smugness to horror. Those of his teammates who knew him well would later claim that they could see his mind working ever more desperately through each one of those possibilities as the ball spiralled menacingly through the air.

Rocket had once had a tennis lesson in which the coach told him to "always play a drop shot with a drop shot" and a process of deduction lead him to the first possibility of playing a soft scoop dig with a soft scoop dig. The trouble was that the ball was going to bounce quite high, rendering his soft-scoop dig even less effective. The high backhand kill quickly presented itself as the next possibility in Rocket's mind but it was just as quickly removed. Still wondering where Mitch was, the final possibility was the one Rocket settled upon. He had seen players on television run round the ball to take it on their forehand and, before it was too late, he set off running sideways and backwards, preparing to play a crunching forehand down the middle, between the helpless Midtown partners.

But a characteristic lack of explosive speed meant that by the time he reached the ball he was positioned for the shot in such a way that there was hardly any room between his nose and the ball to put his racket. In some desperation and now falling backwards with the momentum of such an unaccustomed manoeuvre, he swung at the ball. He connected with the ball by the handle of his racket and, instead of a prodigiously powerful forehand winner, he played one of the softest and most delicate shots his teammates had ever seen him play; a shot of which Mitch, wherever he was, would have been proud, even though Mitch would have preferred to use the strings rather than the handle of the racket. The shot was also one which gave a whole new meaning to 'taking the pace off the ball' as it moved over the net at a speed of no more than three miles per hour and at an angle no one, least of all Rocket, could possibly have anticipated, leaving the Midtown opponents transfixed as they watched the delicate parabola of its flight as it passed slowly in front of them, clipped the top of the net and parachuted into the far tramlines for a clean winner.

Had he seen it, Rocket would have commended himself for his eventual shot selection but he continued to fall back, finally learning the whereabouts of his partner Mitch, who had slipped to the ground going for the shot, by collapsing on top of him. Pausing only to wonder why three of his four Long Shott teammates had handkerchiefs stuffed in their mouths, he asked plaintively, "Did the bugger go in?" Unable to speak, they nodded. Rocket and Mitch stood up proudly and proceeded to the next point with renewed self-belief in their collective skills.

Now Rocket's confidence knew no bounds. He prepared to serve for the match and aimed to deliver an ace from his first serve. Recalling the story about himself in the Evening News, he hit it with the kind of ferocity which would have again taken it into the neighbouring Bowls Club but this time it also had the kind of accuracy which would have kept it not only in the court but in the service box too. The serve had ace written all over it. That is, of course, until it struck Mitch on the back of the head.

Mitch, ever the reliable partner, did not move, imagining perhaps that he had been struck by what certainly felt like a low-flying seagull, the ball came back from his head at a even faster pace and landed in the court behind them. Rocket looked to his team-

-mates for encouragement but they were only to be seen rotating handkerchiefs ferociously inside their mouths. One seemed to be biting on his forefinger; another had implemented a whole-body rocking motion whilst the Club Secretary rolled quietly on his back in the grass verge. Rocket, who looked a little disgruntled to say the least that Mitch had got in the way of a certain ace, momentarily registered that "with supporters like this..." and duly proceeded to deliver an ace on his second serve. This was just as well because Mitch, still stunned, had not moved his position and was patently not in any condition to assist.

Rocket looked up at 15-0 and saw that Mitch had still not moved and was standing at the net on the deuce side of the court. His opponents looked ready so Rocket decided to pretend this was a deliberate plan to play the 'Australian' formation. Mitch was more or less standing in the correct position and although he had begun to rub both his eyes and his racket was placed between his legs, Rocket decided to unleash another big serve while he felt the force was with him. Ace. 30-0. Rocket changed sides quickly and took a quick glance at Mitch. Mitch was still in the same place but was now back in the normal position and better still, had his racket back in his hands. So without pausing to find a second ball, Rocket delivered another fuel-injected serve which swung wide to the forehand side for another ace. 40-0. Triple match point.

At this point, Mitch had regained enough consciousness to move from the point of impact but he still didn't feel too good and consequently only made it two steps to his right before feeling a little dizzy. To stop him losing his balance, he decided to squat down in the middle of the court, using his racket as a kind of stick to lean against. By this time Rocket had picked up another ball. Recognising that Mitch's position could be interpreted as 'the tandem formation', he unleashed another ferocious serve. This time, it hit the opponent's strings with a mighty shuddering clout and floated back towards Mitch. Fortunately, Mitch's dizzy spell had passed and he naturally began to stand up at the exact time the ball came towards him, ending the match with an easy kill.

The team supporters clapped wildly and cheered loudly, happy both for the win and for the fact that they could now let the repressed laughter escape, masked as cheers.

Thus Long Shott Men's Team eventually won this crucial tie and returned home even more confident that they might also avoid relegation next year. Having been told by everyone than he really can 'handle' it, without realising the pun, Rocket's commitment is growing and in the winter months, silhouettes of Rocket have been sighted against the skyline of the Spin Valley Fells earnestly practising half-decent low to high backhands.

# E-COACH

*Tennis hasn't changed too much in the twenty first century but the way we communicate has changed. Some coaches have had trouble adapting to the new media....*

### PART 1: SLOW COACH

Robert Speed was not convinced that putting twenty second videos on *YouTube* of drive volleys or overhead smashes, draped with advertisements for dental floss, new varieties of dog chew or cheap car hire firms in Southern Spain necessarily led to better execution of the shots. And he was not convinced that 'tweeting' about what you are currently doing at any one instant in time led to the edification of anything and, to him, only appeared to serve the self-promotion of the coach or player. Why would anybody be helped by knowing that at 8.15 a.m. he had just had a bagel and cream cheese and was now on his way to warm-up with two of his hitting partners called Jake and Findlay? He was not convinced that posting personal information, pictures and regular updates about yourself brought you any closer to the younger players you were coaching.

Robert Speed was not the ideal e-coach. But at his interview at the Long Shott Tennis Club - linked to the North West Regional Tennis Centre-where he would oversee both coaching for the members and junior player development, he reassured the interview panel of his outstanding credentials in this regard. Yes, he was 'IT-literate'... And yes, not only could he handle all the new communications media with ease, he could also down and upload digital video coaching sequences, and yes, definitely, he could use *YouTube* and was writing an e-book on 'how to win tennis matches patiently'. He convinced the panel. His mugging up of all the necessary jargon obviously worked.

Privately, as we know, the story was a bit different.

Robert liked to do things slowly. He believed in a patient, measured approach to tasks. He distrusted the pace of modern life with its liking for all that was instant. Instant coffee. Instant messaging. Instant response. People complained about being money rich but time-poor. He was happy to remain relatively money-poor but time-rich. He positively revelled in all that was slow. He loved steam trains, writing letters in long-hand and taking long, aimless ambles in the country. Recently he had become enthusiastic about the principles of the slow-food movement which had, he learned, grown up in Italy and was based in the time-honoured and proven methods of home cooking, where pasta and bread was cooked or baked daily and where the human hand was at work in the process of preparation. A world without microwaves, without ready meals, without 'just-heat-it-up-and-enjoy-fresh-from-the-farm goodness.' Bliss.

His approach to coaching the junior players in his charge was the same: 'you learn to play the game by being dedicated and by paying attention to detail. It is a slow process and sometimes you have to go backwards before you can go forward.' Slowly. Robert positively enjoyed being behind the curve, off the pace, in the slow lane. He also believed that this was good for his players. He was a slow coach.

He was a little uncertain about all new technologies which must, he concluded, inevitably speed things up. If the great players of the past learned the game by being shown, face to face, patiently and slowly and then practised and practised, why would a player today need a coach with a web-site? It is all a matter of getting the fundamentals right and the fundamentals don't change.

It might be thought that with such an approach to coaching he would not be very popular. But the parents of his coaching charges loved him. Many of them shared, almost nostalgically, an appreciation of his slow, patient, old school methods. They too despaired of the call from their child for the very latest (and often more expensive) piece of technology, always prefixed by an i- or an e-. And they didn't mind paying Robert the higher fees he charged for individual and group lessons, as they believed (probably incorrectly) that he actually saved them money by discouraging these new technologies.

The trouble was that in his role as a regional coach, responsible for coach and Under 14 player development, Robert was coming under increasing pressure to communicate instantly with others by mobile phone, text and skype and to make use of the facilities for 'posting' coaching examples on the web.

Robert was not unaware of this conflict of interest. Indeed ten years ago, just as other coaches were discovering the value of digital cameras and web-enabled reviewing, Robert prided himself on his investment in a video-camera loaded with little 30 minute tapes that took an eternity to load, even longer to play back and required the patience of a Cambodian monk before they were developed and stored on his home video recorder (at that time he thought portable DVDs and laptops 'gimmicky'). By the time he had one of his players round to his house to watch the video, the point of the lesson was long lost and Robert had to start all over again with the demonstration of the technique.

As the pressure on him increased, however, he invested in a mobile phone (though made sure it was always switched off) so he could play back and listen to messages before carefully composing his reply. The phone could handle email and texts which he found just about acceptable but complained that the size of the keyboard and his own meticulous concern for correct spelling, punctuation and paragraphing meant that he was constantly correcting his own compositions. As a result it did take him longer to communicate through his phone than by most other means of communication and, although he often joked that handwriting a note and posting it in a post box was probably quicker, he was at least, as he would say: "IT-literate."

But his national tennis federation did not just leave it there. To connect with young players these days, it was essential for the coach to embrace the technologies that were part of the fabric of the daily lives of the players. And, predictably enough, he had only been in the job six months when he was invited to attend a course on:

**Social networking in Tennis:**
**New Pathways for Player and Coach Development.**

The course lasted four days (one day would have been sufficient Robert felt) and during this time no-one even touched a tennis racket or ball. He came back with a splitting head ache from staring continually at small screens.

Follow-up monitoring and 'support' sessions were held and he was initially encouraged to communicate electronically with club members. On each occasion Robert didn't quite pull it off.

**Speed text**
After a couple of weeks back at Long Shott and after several follow-up texts from the Social Networking course support team Robert collected all the phone numbers of the members of his coaching groups and started sending texts to his Cardio Tennis group.

**Text 1 (Sept 28)**
Dr all,
Jst 2 say high. Soz, I mean hi, Rob.

**Text 2 (Sept 30)**
Tmrw (i.e. tomorrow) plse meet at ate (i.e.eight) not 4. That is 8 not 4. Rob.

Robert never quite trusted the shorthand of texting but as he got more confident he began to experiment.

**Text 3 (Oct 7)**
4 cardio prep tmrw don't forget 2 all bring sm rpe w u so we can make a lder 2 to do drls.

The last text occasioned replies from all his class who wanted to know what 'lder' or 'rpe' and 'drl' were. Two of them phoned to say his text was indecipherable. One phoned the club to complain, saying that she thought it was in a foreign language and that Robert was making fun of them all.

### Text 4 (Oct 8)

Soz, all. I mean, please accept my apologies. Please bring some rope with you to our next class so that we can make a ladder to do the stepping drills.

Not practising that much, Robert had by now forgotten how to send multiple texts and, of course, sent each one individually. It took him nearly an hour and he kept correcting the spelling in case there were any more misunderstandings.

He was not convinced that texting led to effective communication. He began to wonder if, as he had always done, just getting the club secretary to leave a phone message might not be a lot easier and quicker. He decided to set up a coaching blog instead.

### Speed Blog

Welcome to Rob Speed's tennis blog. This is a fun blog for all interested in tennis. There'll be news, gossip, opinions, photos of matches, updates on our local players and coaching advice, humorous tennis stories, jokes, equipment reviews and details of tennis holidays. Stay tuned. There's a lot about to come your way.

Let's begin the first fun blog with coaching advice.

### How to hit a slice serve in ten fun steps

1. Stand six feet from the net.

2. Hold the racquet by the bottom of its throat, using a Continental grip.

3. While holding the ball in your left hand (for righties), practice brushing your strings across the right side of the ball (from the centre toward 3:00 on an imaginary clock face).

4. Hold your racquet with your elbow bent so that the racquet head is almost touching your upper back.

5. Toss the ball one foot higher than your head, around 18 inches straight to your right, and strike the ball by brushing across its back, from the centre toward 3:00.

6. Practice with this choked-up grip and small toss until you can see the ball spinning around its vertical axis as it goes over the net. Don't worry about getting it into the service box.

7. Take a giant step back. Slide your hand an inch closer to the end of your handle.

8. Toss a few inches higher and an inch or two farther to your right and strike the ball as before.

9. Practice from this position until you can get the ball over the net and see its sidespin.

10. Now try to get the ball into the service box from the baseline.

Fun eh? Hope you enjoyed this first blog. Stay in touch.

Robert's first blog was removed from the club's website when, after trying to follow Robert's instructions, two club players fell backwards and one damaged a shoulder. After two weeks no-one claimed to have progressed in their use of the slice serve.

Robert received only one comment in reply from the husband of one of his Cardio Tennis group members. "Sounds great fun, Rob!!! But where's all the news and gossip? Couldn't see any jokes?!"

## PART 2: GETTING MUCH QUICKER
### *Twitter Speed*

It was a fine June day and Robert was sitting on his balcony enjoying freshly squeezed orange juice and a farm-reared bacon sandwich in bread that he had prepared in his own oven (and which he was consuming very slowly) when he was interrupted by the ominous ping of his mobile phone. He eventually sneaked a look and read the following message:

> Robert,
>
> We are at stage 3 in our research into the value of new technologies and coaching and have selected you to partake in our latest exploration of the value of Twitter to support player development. Please go to Twittenrol.com where we have prepared a special experimental website for you to communicate with a select group of 14 year olds. The challenge is for you to devise ways of using the unique technological space that Twitter provides to communicate tips and coaching advice with a personal touch.
>
> Please feel free to communicate with the players in a personal way and do not hold back with information about yourself. We want our players to get to know members of the national coaching team as people and feel that coaching should be about friendly, personal support available at any time, on the instant.

You will see from the notes that accompany this research that, in keeping with the scope of Twitter, the challenge for you is to gather as many 'followers' as you can. There will be an initial group of 20 followers and we will be interested to see if you can extend this list as the players in this group pass on your details to other junior players and they become your followers.

You will see that there is also a space in our website for you to add your own comments on the value of this exercise to your own coach development. We are confident that you will have only positive things to report to us.

Thank you for your participation.

The National Tech Coaching Squad.
Follow us on Quicktech@twittenrol.com

Robert felt that he had no choice but to give this a go. He drafted his first post:

Ecoach16@nattennis. Use the drive volley to end a point quickly. Just had a bowl of golden mornings. Lots fibre, helps stamina. Just taking max my dog for a walk.

He wondered whether it might have been better if he had started with the more personal information but he decided to log on and post it.

Nothing happened but after a couple of hours his phone began to ping more frenetically than usual. He had followers; over twenty, in fact. Obviously, the word had got out about his tweets. He felt pleased with himself and, as an advocate of the well-judged drive volley, expected a flurry of comments and reactions.

By the end of the day he was being followed by another two. He couldn't quite decipher who they all were but assumed that they were all linked in some way into the National Tech Squad. By this time he even had replies and comments from a couple of the followers:

Ecoach16@nattennis RT dave@tramlines. Yeah, but golden mornings are rubbish. Try chocobix.

Ecoach16@nattennis. RT mikey@bigserve. Stick to wheatbites man.

Much encouraged by the dialogue that was being established, he posted again early the following day.

Ecoach 16@nattennis. Max my dog loves chasing tennis balls. Several all now chewed up. Just squeezed a couple of fresh oranges for lunch. The successful drive volley depends on court position and on watching the ball carefully and particularly on...

Robert tried several times to complete the sentence. He wanted to say 'on taking the ball at shoulder height' but he had used up his 140 characters and writing anything more simply produced dots. He decided that it was best to leave it as it may encourage members of the coaching squads to complete the sentence with their own understandings of the drive volley.

His post today produced one response.

> Ecoach@nattennis RT jill@shortshorts4tennis. Yuk. Fresh
> orange juice.
> Squeeze my pips.

He also noted that the number of his 'followers' had dropped from 22 to 8.

Robert decided that this whole idea was perhaps not the best way to engage with players but, following his philosophy of patience as the way to success and knowing that everything is best done slowly, decided to slow things down for a while and try again in a few days time (even though he kept receiving messages from the National Tech Coaching squad, noting that he had fallen seriously behind the average 12 tweets a day of his fellow coaches).

> Ecoach@nattennis. My dog max loves golden mornings.
> So there. Haha. The stop volley should always be played
> with soft hands. Keep the ball well in front of you and
> glide the racket....Where? Answers please.

Robert waited for the ping of his phone, eagerly anticipating the answer to his technical question but by the end of the day there was nothing and the number of his followers had dropped to one.

The following morning Robert received an email thanking him

for his participation and reporting that the National Tech Coaching Squad were re-evaluating the scheme and were temporarily continuing with just two coaches who were working with them on using social networking to demonstrate biomechanics. He started to feel that maybe he was yesterday's coach. A slow coach.

### PART 3: VERY SLOW SPEED.

The email came as something of a relief to Robert and he took consolation in the fact that this had all been implemented too quickly, that technology moved too fast, paid insufficient attention to detail and failed to reproduce the benefits of face-to-face human contact and coaching. He walked out into his garden, threw an old tennis ball for his dog Max, returned to his kitchen and started to prepare the bread mix for the following day.

He watched a couple of clips from a video of one of his players missing a drive volley at a key point in a match and made notes in pencil in his coaching book, mentally rehearsing how he would find the best ways of getting the message across to his pupil tomorrow morning; how he would encourage him to get to the net more by using the example of Max the dog and his continual alertness to where the ball is. Robert noted that the coaching sequence would need to be repeated over the next few weeks to ensure that it was properly retained. It would be a slow process.

# HOME ADVANTAGE

*An administrative error results in a Junior Federation Cup match being played in East Borne in Spin Valley. With Tibetan monks humming in the stand and ball girls causing chaos, an eventful match heads towards an exciting climax.*

As soon as the Great Britain Women's Coach heard they had drawn Spain at home in the Junior Federation Cup, her mind turned to 'home advantage'. The Spanish have a strong reputation for tennis but it was not developed on soft, slightly damp grass courts.

In a hurry to get to an important selection meeting, she asked the temporary secretary to check that the grass courts at Devonshire Park, Eastbourne were available on the allotted day. "The phone number's in the handbook." she shouted on her way out of the office.

Devonshire Park had just upgraded their stadium on the centre court and although the new temp didn't know it, Eastbourne and its tennis facilities had a strong tradition in women's international tennis; East Borne Tennis Club in Spin Valley did not. They were, however, very proud of their two grass courts which they leased from the council in Dorset Park. So when the club secretary, Mrs Slade-Lipkin, received a phonecall to check on their availability for a Junior Federation Cup tie against Spain from an albeit slightly hesitant and confused young girl, she became very excited.

Mrs Slade-Lipkin immediately formed a working party. They discussed what holding the event might entail - local accommodation, a stand for spectators, catering, ticket sales, the training of ball-girls… The most important thing was, however, to notify the local council and the press.

East Borne is a small market town in Spin Valley, near Dipton, below Edendale. Except for the summer livestock show, it rarely gets much publicity. The decision to hold a junior international tennis match there attracted widespread interest and not inconsiderable curiosity from the press. Mrs Slade-Lipkin was very pleased with the immediate coverage the story received; The Great Britain Women's Team Coach was not. Few temporary secretaries have ever been so temporary.

In the ensuing days there were many diplomatically made phone calls, received most undiplomatically. The bottom line was that East Borne Town Council was delighted to have been asked to stage the prestigious event and could not possibly accept any change of heart now. Eventually, after much discussion, a delegation travelled up from London to check that the grass courts were soft and damp enough. The decision stood and Spin Valley prepared to hold its first ever international tennis match.

As the big day drew closer, many of the meticulously planned preparations were put in place, under the direction of the formidable Mrs Slade-Lipkin, who also took charge of personally selecting and training the ball-girls.

The ball-girls were chosen from the local school and trained in the school sports hall. Mrs Slade-Lipkin had been sent instructions on how to train ball-girls up to international standard. After the first six sessions were spent teaching the girls to roll a tennis ball in something like a straight line, she decided the whole thing was more complicated than it looked. Most of the girls were badly co-ordinated, didn't concentrate and had never even played tennis. She decided to pick the six most promising candidates and try to teach them the basics.

With about a week to go, she had just about taught them where to stand (one in either corner of the court and two squatting at net) and the golden rule that the girls at the net should never pass the balls directly to the player but should instead roll them to the girls at the back, who should then throw them to the players.

Unfortunately, the last crucial sessions, which might have reinforced what little the girls had learnt, had to be cancelled when a crisis arose. In the excitement of being asked to host the match, no-one had actually arranged to book the courts and somehow, in the interim, someone from the local council had booked out the clubhouse for the week to be used by a group of two hundred Tibetan monks. They had been attracted to the area by its remoteness, peace and outstanding natural beauty. The monks needed the clubhouse for meditation and had also booked the two courts so that they would not be disturbed by the sound of tennis balls being hit. Under any normal circumstances, this would be quite acceptable as at East Borne, Spin Valley, the non-tennis income often outstripped the income generated by tennis. In the winter it was not unusual for the grasscourts to be hired out to local farmers to graze their prize-winning goats on.

It was impossible to even consider the possibility of revealing the oversight to the L.T.A. but at the same time, turning the Tibetan monks away at this late stage was not possible either. Furthermore, the monks were undertaking a period of silence and could not be contacted. The crisis was settled with only two days to go, when the Tibetan monks eventually phoned to confirm their arrival time. After much explanation, they agreed to have a day less indoors and accepted free tickets to watch the match, as long as they could continue some form of meditation while they watched.

The Spanish team arrived at Spin Valley Airport the day before the match in good spirits. Their first inkling that it was going to be a difficult weekend came when they were met at the airport by the Official Transportation Manager, Arkwright Stone and his thirty-five-year old sheep truck. The five hour journey north was comfortable enough for the Spanish team coach in the front but for the three players sat in the back of the truck with the two Suffolk-cross ewes Arkwright had just picked up from Stoneshire, the journey was far from pleasant. Needless to say they did not feel quite up to practising when they finally arrived in East Borne.

Mrs Slade-Lipkin had consulted with the town council about the type of accommodation the Spanish team might like and they had decided upon a traditional farmhouse bed and breakfast so they could experience the true country charm of Spin Valley. They so wanted to show the visitors generosity and good hospitality. However, the good intentions of hosts can often go astray. The Spaniards saw little charm in the cold stainless steel showers, little hospitality in the 5 a.m. cockerel and little generosity in the extra 'Shott sausage' served with the cooked breakfast.

It was, though, a nice bright morning as they travelled to the courts in the sheep truck. The sun shone from a clear blue sky where paragliders could be seen floating around admiring the view. Practice didn't go too badly and things seemed to be picking up when cold paella was served for lunch.

Ticket sales had gone well and, including the Tibetan monks, there were four hundred and fifty spectators in the stands. The first two matches were both excellent with the lead changing hands several times. Great Britain had won the first by mid-afternoon but the Spanish had levelled at 1-1 by tea time. As the third and deciding match went on, there was not a free seat in the stand.

The Spanish girl, Maria, looked ill at ease; she had never played a match on grass before and even in between the points she constantly kept an eye on it as if she mistrusted it. She was unnerved by the Tibetan monks who, rather than clapping, hummed after good rallies. Furthermore, the sun had faded, the temperature had dipped and there was a dewy feel to the air. Had she been more at ease, she may not have noticed the ball-girls. However, her irritable attention was drawn to them early on, when, after she double faulted into the net, the ball-girl ran, collected the ball, slipped and skidded across the damp grass on her stomach in a superman position.

She next served at 0-2 down and turned to get a ball from the ball-girl at the back of the court. Maria nodded at her but the ball-girl just stood, holding the ball above her head with a straight arm. She nodded again but again nothing happened. She turned away to face the other ball-girl and hoped for a better response. What she didn't realise was that, by the second nod, the first ball-girl had actually registered what a nod meant and any further delay was only caused by the muscles in her arm processing precisely what her brain was requesting. Just as the Spanish girl turned away, the ball-girl threw the ball down. The ball bounced up on one of the few hard patches of grass and hit Maria squarely in the face. From here things went from bad to worse.

At 2-4, the Spaniard turned again for a ball from the ball-girl at the back but instead had to wait for all the balls to be rolled up from the other end. Already impatient, Maria was far from pleased, when the balls finally arrived, that the girl had completely forgotten her training and had rolled them back in the direction they had just travelled. Maria tried to short cut the process by walking to the girl at the net and demanding the ball with an angry motion. However, the girl at the net knew the golden rule and was not prepared to break it. Maria saw her intention and, holding her finger out menacingly as a warning, edged slowly forwards and sideways to cut off the way to the ball-girl at the back. The girl at the net thought quickly and wrong-footed the Spaniard by rolling the balls diagonally across the court to the other ball-girl at the back. As Maria recovered her balance and dived to try to intercept the third ball, the girl at the net dummied a rolling action and then propelled it quickly down the line to first girl at the back. It was then that Maria cracked her first racket and received her first warning. The Tibetan monks hummed softly and an eerie, misty, low cloud began to settle around the park.

At 6-3 to Great Britain a ball change was due. The ball-girls performed admirably, collecting the old balls quickly into the cans. They then took the old balls back out of the cans and redistributed them around the court. It took a further three minutes to get the old balls back in and the new balls out. Finally, Maria stood holding the new balls and tried to compose herself for the now vital start of the second set. Strong words were shouted in very fast Spanish from the coach at the side of the court. She responded well and played with renewed purpose, quickly collecting any loose balls near her between points so she could maintain her momentum. This worked well and she raced to a 3-0 lead. Yet she now had to be as sharp in between the points as she was during them, because the ball-girls were also getting quicker in reaching the loose balls.

At 3-1, she was twice just beaten to a loose ball by the ball-girls and her momentum was interrupted. This clearly affected her rhythm and she lost the game to go 3-2. She regained her composure and changed ends four games later at 5-4 up. This game was particularly hard fought and the high standard of play was reflected in the amount of clapping and humming from the crowd. The Spaniard reached set point at 40-30 and moved quickly after a loose ball. She could see a ball-girl from the back approaching quickly out of the corner of her eye and so quickly lunged, bringing her racket down sharply to claim ownership of the ball. Unfortunately the ball-girl's hand got there first and as the racket struck her fingers she let out a piercing screech of pain.

There was a five minute delay while the ball-girl left the court with blood dripping from her hand. There was a further five minute delay while the remaining ball-girl at the back was stretchered off, having fainted at the sight of the blood. The Spaniard didn't win another point that game but seemed to regain composure at 5-5, calmed by the fact that there were now no ball-girls behind her and she could finally pick up her own balls.

At this stage, the ball-girl at the net did what no ball-girl or boy should ever risk doing; she showed initiative. In the absence of anyone at the back and a ball loose at 30-30, she ran, collected it from the back and returned to the net. Maria once again came forward menacingly. The ball-girl stayed as still as a statue. She was in a fix this time. She couldn't break the golden rule but there was nobody at the back to roll it to. After a thirty second stand off (during which even the humming stopped) and several shouts from the ball girl trainer Mrs Slade-Lipkin, the girl reluctantly passed the ball to the Spaniard.

By this time Maria's composure was gone again and she changed ends at 5-6 down. In the next game the British girl forced her way to match point with some fine play. The rally at match point was breath-taking with the Spanish girl pushing the British girl from side to side. After twenty eight shots the British girl retrieved an impossible ball, skidding to the ground as she did so. With her opponent stranded, Maria whipped the ball towards the gap. The ball hit the top of the net which took most of the pace out of it but still it span forward and upward slowly, towards the open court. Reacting quickly, the ball girl nearest the net moved gracefully to take the ball out of the air before it bounced. Had the ball-girl at the net known the rules of tennis, she may never have taken the finest catch of her life.

It was then that the Spaniard cracked her second racket. The match point was replayed according to the rules. The Spanish girl didn't even move as the British girl served a clean ace. Too cold to clap, the whole crowd hummed with approval. The British team were carried off on the shoulders of their supporters, gave many press interviews and celebrated until the small hours.

It was indeed a historic day. Britain had beaten Spain for the first time in fifteen years, several of the crowd had converted to Buddhism and Spin Valley had given a whole new meaning to the words 'home advantage'.

# THE COURT

It's not exactly fast or slow,
Not grass, nor hard, nor clay,
It's not that strictly by the rules,
It's officially fit for play.

It's a different type of hard court,
Been repaired from patch to patch,
With different types of tarmac,
For a different type of match.

Its net can let a ball through,
A basketball in fact,
Its fence is kind of shipwrecked,
Its lines are mostly cracked.

It suits my one-off hit-miss game,
And my mis-matched patchwork kit,
It's weathered like my chipped return
And my cross court drop miss-hit.

It may well suit your game style,
If you choose your place to play,
The far back downhill backhand court,
Is where you'll find the clay.

There's clumps of grass in the service box,
If you're Wimbledon at heart,
Though if you have an all-court game,
You'll not know where to start.

You may prefer the uphill end,
Depending on the rain,
Coz the cracks around your service line,
Give the stream a place to drain.

It's at its best in the wind and rain,
With a player who plays indoors,
Who's never seen this type of court,
With so many different floors.

A player with a silky swing path,
Who prefers a bounce that's true,
Who finds it hard to time the ball,
Where the roots are breaking through.

Hit that spot in the service box,
For a sure-fire clean-roll ace;
Or the moss up by the baseline,
Then watch your opponent's face.

And if the first set doesn't go too well.
Don't be down at heart,
Coz with tennis and the broken bits,
It's never too late to start.

They'll give you hope of turning points,
When your back's against the wall,
A lucky bounce escape route,
From a last-ditch hacked-back ball.

A chance to turn the tables,
To turn the match around,
From a floaty flicked-back flightpath,
That falls on stoney ground.

Coz it favours those who view it,
With an eye for a lucky patch,
So challenge those who play indoors,
And plan you're greatest match.

# LONG SHOTT

## TENNIS CLUB'S GRASS COURT CHAMPIONSHIPS

*The weather has conspired against both the French Open and a Spin Valley groundsman's plan to keep his grass courts 'unfit for play.' Consequently, a large crowd watches the final of the Annual Grass Court Championships, (surprisingly played on grass) and is entertained by Rocket, who is playing in the final against Mitch, stumbling from one disaster to another.*

Long Shott Tennis Club has two Championships each year. The Hard Court Championships and the Grass Court Championships. The Annual Grass Court Championships are not actually held at the club. They are held in a nearby sports ground in Clopton, also in Spin Valley.

At this sports ground there are reputed to be three of the finest grass courts in the country. This claim was a little difficult to prove as the groundsman rarely allows anyone to play on them. This was particularly the case during the Annual Grass Court Championships.

Most of the matches took place on the adjoining cement, concrete or clay courts whilst the grass courts stood immaculate but empty. However, if you played your match on the clay, it could be argued that grass court tactics were in part appropriate, due to the clumps of coarse grass growing in the service boxes.

Reasons for the unavailability of the grass courts varied but were essentially the same:
"No play before 11 a.m. - courts too soft because of dew."
"No play after 5 p.m. - courts too soft because of dew."
"No play in the early rounds of the tournament - courts should

not be too worn for Finals Day." "No play on Finals Day - courts too soft due to under use."

If you travelled to nearby Clopton to play in their Championships, the grass was likely to be greener on the other side of the fence.

Each year a large crowd would come to the ground to watch the tennis and prior to the final, the bar at the sports ground was usually buzzing. But the crowd stayed in the bar. They had not come to watch the Club Championships. They had come to watch The French Open final which was played at the same time every year. The Clopton sports ground bar has the only satellite television for miles around.

The year of the tennis club centenary was different. Due to a lapse on the part of the French weather system, the French Open was postponed for the day and due to a lapse on the part of the groundsman, the grass courts were fit for the finals. The large French Open crowd waited for a while in the bar and then turned their attention from Paris to Clopton and drifted outside to watch the Men's Singles Final.

Some things in Spin Valley never change and for the ninth year in a row the final was being played between Mitch and Rocket. As ever, the match was hard fought and closely contested.

From Rocket's point of view, the match was progressing relatively well at 3-3 in the first set. Mitch had hardly moved to intercept any of his ferocious first serves. Furthermore, he was dealing well with Mitch's normally tricky sliced serve and had even had three break points already. In fact, Rocket felt sure he would have already secured a break, if he had not been distracted on a vital smash by local farmer Arkwright Stone and his son Clegg, ostentatiously practising on the back cement courts, three courts distance to the left behind the line of grass courts. Indeed, Arkwright and Clegg were not only distracting Rocket but also the spectators who were now swollen to around the size of a legion of French deserters.

It would be a trusting sort indeed who believed that Arkwright could practice so loudly and be innocently unaware of the attention of the hundred or so people less than a hundred yards away. Arkwright was in his element and although he gave a credible impression of someone simply getting on with the job of coaching his son, he was showing off with every action and with every word that was powerfully shouted to Clegg, despite him being only five yards away. Arkwright took particular pride in explaining his philosophies and his work ethic and continued to act as if oblivious to the nearby final.

Fortunately the match was exciting and as 4-4 turned to 5-5, 30-all, a hushed, concentrated silence descended upon the crowd so that no-one noticed Arkwright demonstrating smashes to his son. Mitch was serving. Surely this time he had to aim for Rocket's backhand - the crowd sensed it and so did Rocket. However Mitch went for an ace to the forehand and struck it well. Rocket, though, somehow one bluff ahead, moved early and had time on the ball. Never before on a tennis court in Spin Valley had so much weight moved with such momentum, a racket travelled so fast, or a ball been hit so cleanly.

The crowd watched in awe as Rocket's forehand flew over the net and continued to fly. It was rising as it flew over the incoming Mitch's head, rising as it crossed the baseline and still rising as it went over the fence at the back left of the court.

Time stood still as everyone's eyes followed the ball and its destined flight path. As the ball began to descend, one hundred pairs of eyes fell on Arkwright. He was still demonstrating smashes and, as if sensing everyone was watching, puffed out his chest, tilted his head proudly and focused intently on the ball his son had just lobbed for him. Had he not been quite so intently focused on this ball, he might have spotted Rocket's ball hurtling towards him at 45 degrees from the left. It was precisely at this point that everyone discovered Arkwright wore a toupee as Rocket's ball hit it with such force that even industrial staples wouldn't have held it on.

Rocket's ball knocked Arkwright to the ground. Arkwright quickly rose to his feet, briefly glancing upwards to see what could have possibly hit him so hard. This was a serious mistake as just then, the ball lobbed by his son moments earlier came hurtling down and struck him in the eye. The concentrated tension of the watching crowd was broken as everyone tried various unsuccessful ways to stop laughing. Everyone that was, except Rocket.

Anger welled up inside him as he turned to slam a ball into the back fence. Several of the crowd saw what was coming and ducked. One of them was the referee who, in trying to take avoiding action, threw his cup of tea over Mrs Slade-Lipkin. Rocket belted the ball at the fence. The ball rebounded with equal force off a post and shot back to hit him in the groin. At the same time the pole snapped and the whole back stop fencing came down, snapping the other poles along the line of courts on its descent before landing on top of the doubled-over Rocket.

Few were in a position to come to Rocket's aid. The referee had to attend to Mrs Slade-Lipkin, the groundsman was in a state of shock staring at the marks on his grass courts and everyone else was crossing the pain barrier with a sustained period of suppressed laughter. Rocket did finally receive medical attention, but he had to retire injured. When things had eventually settled down, the rest of the finals were completed in a less dramatic and certainly more traditional fashion......on the clay courts.

The events of the centenary year of the Grass Court Championships were thus a landmark in the history of the event. Never again would the groundsman let Rocket play on the grass, never again would Arkwright and Clegg practice on courts while Rocket was playing nearby and never again would the good people of Clopton assume that the French Open had better spectator value than the Annual Grass Court Championships.

# OVERHEADS TO PAY

L.S. T.C.

LONG SHOTT TENNIS CLUB
*Since 1876*

ENTHUSIASTICUS
DESPITUS
ELEMENTUM

He's not happy going forward,
The net's a dangerous place,
His basic plan is backward,
Retreat then turn and face.

Coz he likes to play the lob-shot,
It's the shot he lives to play,
He happiest when he's lobbing,
So he's happy most the day.

He'll hang it on a sky-hook,
Use the sun to blind,
With canny regularity,
He'll land it on the line.

So if you meet him on the match court,
There'll be overheads to pay,
And if your balance isn't good,
You'd better stay away.

# ANOTHER LOB

The grass was artificial,
The rain was coming down,
Another lob was coming,
My partner wore a frown.

Another lob was coming,
My partner stood entranced,
"ANOTHER LOB IS COMING!"
And back he finally danced.

He missed the smash, I didn't mind,
I was used to that by now,
But he didn't see them coming up,
Till they were on their way back down.

I mean lobs is all they dealt in,
It was all their grips allowed,
And thirty-six in the first four games
Should be registering somehow.

Another lob looked likely,
So I threw a glance alongside,
And scrutinised my partner's face,
now what was on his mind?

The look was one of innocence,
Nothing registered yet,
So I had to yell as the ball went up:
"You've got a lob to get!"

So I had a word at the change of ends,
"About these lobs…" I said,
"You could maybe do with spotting them,
Before they've passed your head."

He'll get a grasp of that, I thought,
With him a space cadet,
But the ball flew up to dizzy heights
And he hadn't left the net.

I thought about it long and hard,
And tried a different way,
"There's a hornets' nest in the net post…
It's not the place to stay."

But the lobbers must have guessed the plan,
For then the lobbing stopped,
And with racket faces open,
They began to play drop-shots.

My partner's head was spinning,
He was rooted to the ground,
With hornets' nests and drop shots,
And lobs that didn't come down.

He came to me at the change of ends,
"I've got to stop" he said,
"I'm going home to have a bath,
And then I'm off to bed…

…I've a mortal fear of hornets,
I can't go near that net,
What's more, with all that looking up,
I've gone and cricked mi neck!"

So we packed our bags in silence,
Our clothes were dripping wet,
As a passing wasp flew by,
It stung him on the neck.

# JEFF
## (SPIRITUAL HEAD COACH)
### V
# ARKWRIGHT
## (THE TENNIS FARMER)

*Arkwright knows only one way: 'dig deeper, try harder'... It works on the farm and, after all, tennis is even simpler.*

Arkwright Stone is a farmer. He has four major interests, three of which are shared with all other farmers. The three interests are: his sheep, his cattle and his crops. At one point or other in the year, one or other of his sheep, his cattle or his crops become problems and it is not unusual for them to become problems all at the same time. Given the position and climate of Spin Valley, where it rains sideways, Arkwright has learned that he has to accept rain-rotten crops, BSE in his cows and every disease known to the veterinary profession in his sheep.

Like many farmers Arkwright was built for endurance and you could easily imagine him ramming his way through the opposition in the Axle Motors Spin Valley Floodlit Rugby League. But in his choice of sports Arkwright was different from all other farmers and this was his fourth major interest.

Arkwright was a Long Shott Club third team tennis player. For nearly twenty five years, playing tennis had presented him with opportunities to demonstrate the stoical determination to win through against all the odds which he had learned from his years as a farmer. His team lost many more matches than it won and so Arkwright was presented with regular opportunities to display these qualities. But, in general, tennis was a contrast to his daily life. He might have had problems with his sheep dips and eighteen hours a day lambing was certainly no joke but tennis, he believed, was simple and straightforward.

Arkwright liked things to be straightforward and to reinforce his point, he always refused to fill his truck at garages which sold hot dogs, newspapers, tuna and cucumber rolls, flowers, milk, videos and deep-frozen lean cuisine ready meals. "Garages should just sell petrol." He would say.

Arkwright was determined that his son should succeed and indeed outstrip his achievements in tennis. He devoted many hours to coaching his son at the club which was over five miles away and to which they would regularly jog to improve fitness levels. They lived in the remote village of Dipton, a village which lacked not only tennis facilities but any facilities at all.

Each morning before breakfast Arkwright would have his son, Clegg, serve into a sheep pen, the height of which had been cleverly adjusted to that of a tennis net. He would also get him to make twenty second sprints between serves to develop fitness and second-serve concentration, a task Clegg performed with purple-faced obedience. Although several sheep had leapt over the pen and had had to be retrieved from a rockface on a neighbouring farm, Arkwright knew that his son was a better player for having to come through with home-made facilities.

Arkwright would frequently write to Long Shott Tennis Club bemoaning the lack of support his son received and at the same time berating them for not accepting the offer to other players of his own home-made training facilities. Simple 'grit' and a determination to win against all the odds were lacking in British tennis, he would say. And 'Stuff your new Indoor Tennis Centres' he would always put as a P.S. to his letters.

Arkwright was a big man. It was rumoured that he wore a toupee, parted in the middle and held down with what might have been axle grease. He would always arrive at the tennis club for a father and son coaching session wearing an old, unfashionable tracksuit and carrying a rucksack which contained a racket, a packet of string, three elastoplasts, three old grips, a carrier bag of practice balls, an anorak and a climbing rope (in case they were unable to get back home via the road).

The son, Clegg, had hair parted in the middle and held down with gel. He would arrive for the coaching session wearing an old, unfashionable tracksuit and carrying a rucksack which contained a racket, a packet of string, three elastoplasts, three old grips, a carrier bag of practice balls, an anorak and a climbing rope. He was different from his father only in as far as his tracksuit emitted the unmistakable odour of the cow sheds against whose doors he often practised.

Occasionally, they would be accompanied to coaching sessions by the wife and mother, Morag, who was quiet and demure, half the size of her husband and her son and who would drive to the club in their thirty-five year old sheep truck. She did not carry a rucksack, she did not even play tennis but she did have her hair parted in the middle, kept in place by a strong-hold hairspray. She too always carried a climbing rope with her.

The coaching sessions were always conducted publically and loudly and Arkwright had a habit of arranging his coaching sessions to coincide with important events at the Tennis Club. One key ladies doubles match had to be interrupted because the calls could not be heard above Arkwright's ecstatic shouting at his son's increasingly successful sliced backhand.

Arkwright had taught his son to despise those juniors who were sufficiently distracted from serious tennis to turn up with tennis bags covered with the names of international companies. Only when Clegg once reached the final of the Under 14 Junior Club Tournament, had Arkwright become so drunk that he allowed his son to write NIKE on the side of his rucksack with black marker pen.

As might be expected, Arkwright was an ever-present parent at far away L.T.A Parents meetings and would always ask what the L.T.A could do for his son in Dipton. He was not impressed by eloquent descriptions of the new high-tech indoor facilities in the city of Smogchester, over eighty miles away. "What can the L.T.A do for my son in Dipton?" he would ask on every occasion. "And what can you do for sheepdogs in Smogchester?" an official once retorted in desperation. On another occasion Arkwright went with his son for a sports psychology talk on the importance of playing against your own goals rather than the opponent. He walked out after ten minutes emitting the word "claptrap."

Arkwright knew that indoor tennis made players soft and continued to teach his son the virtues of dogged determination, something he knew could only be developed outside, in inclement conditions (preferably lateral rain) and after five-mile jogs to the nearest tennis court. "Who needs jogging machines with automatic inclines and who wants to row against the blurred outlines of an Olympic rowing team when you can jog up through the mists to the village of Dipton?" he would say.

One day Arkwright received a letter informing him that he had been invited to play in the finals of Regional Veterans Tournament. The post was brought to him by the vet who had just diagnosed foot rot in his sheep and announced that 30% of his flock would have to be destroyed.

Arkwright stoically accepted that he would have to lose his sheep and resolved to win the Veterans tournament. His spirits were soon lifted as he learned that the match was to be played outside, that the weather forecast was for heavy rain and that Jeff Ghandi, his long time rival, was his opponent.

Arkwright spent the next two weeks running harder than ever before around Dipton and staring aggressively at pictures of Jeff in the local tennis magazine. The night before the match he packed an extra climbing rope into his rucksack just in case he needed it. Arkwright knew that this was another chance to show the tennis club hierarchy what could be achieved with 'grit'. And besides, Jeff Ghandi was a vegetarian and Arkwright never had much time for vegetarians.

# JEFF

## (SPIRITUAL HEAD COACH)

*In a region renowned for its cattle farming, Jeff Ghandi, the local Club Coach, is a vegetarian and an 'outsider' in more senses than one. His attempts to retain his veteran's title involve his unique sense of time, a visit to the police station and a cold biriyani.*

Jeff Ghandi was the Head Coach and was known as something of an outsider. He read books on mysticism, went on spiritual training weekends and was a vegetarian.

Jeff's spiritual training also occasionally affected his awareness of time and on several occasions he had been known to serve by throwing a ball in the air only to let it drop without playing it as he continued to stare, enraptured by the timeless beauty of Spin Valley which had taken his eye as the ball reached the top of its arc. This habit brought charges of gamesmanship from opposing teams and the explanation from his own team that eating tofu turned the mind.

Jeff possessed considerable powers of patience and determination. He was the kind of coach who continued coaching through heavy downpours of rain if he felt he hadn't got his point across; Jeff once took 35 minutes from a one hour lesson trying to elicit from his pupil why a particular backhand volley needed to have side spin on it. He had also been known to play a fifty minute tie break with a ten year old to illustrate that patience is one of the great tennis skills which can serve you well throughout your life.

Above all else, Jeff wanted people to learn to play tennis properly so that they could learn to live life better. Ideally, they did this by setting performance goals for themselves to play against. His coaching philosophy took time to be understood by the locals. His methods seemed to fail to instill 'grit' in players.

Parents who had not understood his stress on the importance of learning for oneself have perceived that sometimes only one thing is learned in a lesson lasting a whole hour and a half. Their children have thus been discouraged from asking too many questions and certainly forbidden to ever disagree with Jeff. Some parents even calculated that, at £30 per hour, learning two teaching points in a lesson costs £15 per point. Other parents would complain that he gave poor value for money compared with a ball machine which, at £3 per hour, could offer a whole host of ever changing options and could entertain children rather than make them think and have to answer questions. Other parents would grumble that their children rarely came off court sweating and that Jeff couldn't call himself a 'performance coach' if no-one performed.

One long dark winter's night Jeff was about to set off for the Veteran's Regional Tournament in Dufford when his girlfriend, who was preparing a special Indian meal, asked when he would be back for dinner. The match was scheduled for 6.30 p.m. Jeff had played and beaten his opponent, Arkwright Stone, on many previous occasions and did not anticipate that he would be home later than 8.30 p.m.

# MEAT v VEG

When the match was delayed to 7p.m., there was added adversity for Arkwright; the match was transferred to an indoor court. Arkwright steeled himself and decided to run down every ball, fight for every point and to be simply grittier than Jeff. After all, unlike farming, tennis was simple and uncomplicated.

During the first set, Jeff began to feel that he was up against a different order of opponent than the Arkwright he had played previously. The new Arkwright was different. He was faster, fitter and had obviously discovered new depths of dogged determination. By 8 p.m. Jeff had lost the first set 6-7. He was not playing well, he was not solving performance problems and now knew he was going to be late home. He was a little disconcerted to be the only match playing indoors (three others were on outdoor courts) as he had mentally prepared for an outdoor match under floodlights and had prayed for the uniquely sideways rain which he knew, from innumerable junior coaching sessions, brought out the best in him.

Jeff had two choices: he could go through the second set in more or less the same mode, accept that he would soon be an over 50s veteran and go home for his vegetable biriyani; or he could think this through, alter his tactics and play to achieve a higher level of performance in the next two sets. For Jeff there was no choice and he changed his tactics to playing long-drawn out points with lots of heavy topspin loops.

Arkwright believed he had played the first set as well as any set he had ever played but then, for some reason, Jeff started playing differently, repeatedly hitting high loopy balls to the baseline. Arkwright assumed it was something to do with 'tactics'; his answer was to run even harder and to be even more determined but Jeff kept playing in the same way. At 4-3 down in the second set Arkwright got out one of his climbing ropes and fingered it determinedly instead of drinking from his water bottle.

By 10.00 p.m. the match was one set all. At 10.23 p.m. the other three matches had ended and the referee went home, forgetting the two gladiators locked in combat on the far indoor court. By 11.00 p.m. with the score locked at 4-4, lights started to go off around them on neighbouring courts but such was the intensity of his focus that Jeff only very dimly registered them and he was certainly concentrating elsewhere when a tannoy announcement was made informing any remaining players on the indoor courts that the centre would be closing in ten minutes. In fact, as he worked his way, point by steady point, towards his victory, Jeff could hear applause and believed he could see lights shining ever more brightly on the court.

At 11.23 p.m. and with Jeff at 6-5 and match point up, Jeff finally hit a high looping topspin forehand to Arkwright's backhand and the ball was returned into the net. As he and Arkwright walked down the corridor he allowed himself the satisfaction of imagining winning the whole tournament.

When they reached the entrance to the Tennis Club reception, they found the door was locked and the club was in darkness. They managed to find a phone and called the manager who, rather disgruntled at being woken, told them that the only door which could be opened that wouldn't trigger the alarm was on the far side of the club buildings. The manager also informed them that this particular door hadn't been opened in all the time he had been with the club (over ten years) so was likely to be rather stiff! With this helpful information he briskly hung up to return to his warm bed.

After forty minutes of heaving with brute strength, lubricating the hinges with a bottle of fairy liquid they had found in the club kitchen and simply kicking it, the door remained firmly closed. With Jeff about to set up camp for the night, Arkwright removed his climbing rope (reserved especially for occasions such as these) and set about creating an elaborate pulley system involving an umpire's chair, two singles sticks and a net winder.

It was 12.28 a.m. when they finally broke out of the club house. Emerging into the cold night air, with bags over their shoulders, looking flustered and under pressure (Jeff had started to think about the vegetable biriyani waiting for him), they were more than a little surprised to be dazzled by two very powerful spotlights. For the shortest of moments Jeff imagined that word had got out about the match and the local press and television crews, complete with lighting rigs, had come for an 'on the spot' interview.

The spotlights belonged, however, to the car of two young, rather spotty Dufford policemen who had responded rapidly to the centre's emergency security system. In spite of all their best efforts, Arkwright and Jeff had tripped an alarm inside the clubhouse. The policemen had some difficulty in accepting the claims to innocence of two flustered men carrying bags over their shoulders, a long piece of climbing rope and a broken singles stick, emerging from a locked clubhouse in the small hours of the morning.

The officers decided that Jeff and Arkwright should be taken to the station for further questioning. It was not until 2.30 a.m., a full six and a half hours after he had predicted, that Jeff arrived back at his home. His girlfriend had left instructions for microwaving the meal but warned him not to microwave the naan bread as it would go soggy.

By 2.50 a.m. and eating very soggy, warm naan bread and cold biriyani, Jeff Ghandi had started to prepare mentally for his next Veteran's match. But he also began to think that it was even more important for his pupils to develop the life skills of greater patience, good preparation and a personal-goal setting mentality. He decided that from now on all his coaching sessions would be of two hours duration.

Since losing the Veteran's match, Arkwright has not been seen so often in Spin Valley tennis circles. However, Clegg has been seen, sporting an Afro hair-style and driving a girlfriend around the region in a ten year-old sheep truck. Clegg was rumoured to be specialising in sports science and psychology in Smogchester, working out every day in a gym and playing inter-college tennis at ever higher levels. Arkwright has been seen jogging through the mists in the heights of Dipton but according to the local vet, is now digging even deeper and devoting all his energy to writing applications for EEC grants for persistent crop failure. He never leaves home without his rucksack and a piece of climbing rope.

# LESSONS OF TENNIS

WOOOSH!!

*A web of Chinese whispers badly affect the performances of Long Shott Tennis Club's ladies teams. In the middle is Alison Scott, an adult improver, unaware of the problems she is causing.*

For five years Alison Scott had played tennis twice a week with the same group of ladies on Tuesday and Thursday mornings. Two hours doubles followed by one hour of coffee was a successful formula. She played at the Middleside Tennis Club where these morning sessions of organised play were very popular. There were often forty or more ladies who turned up.

Very few of these ladies had ever had formal coaching but over coffee they had built up their own ideas on how tennis should be played, based on what they could remember from school, the various *YouTube* clips they religiously watched and good common sense. All the ladies had collectively agreed that, ideally, the ball should skim the net on every shot and indeed even during a rally they would regularly call out 'good shot' if the ball stayed very low as it crossed the net. They developed the idea that for maximum strength the racket should be held in a death grip with the whites of your knuckles showing. Finally and perhaps most importantly, they believed that on no account should a player ever enter "no man's land" in the centre of the court. It certainly seemed to work as the club's four ladies teams always finished high in the Spin Valley Leagues.

Alison was a little different from everyone else at the mornings; she was mainly interested in the tennis and not concerned with the coffee and the chat. The other ladies targeted her for gentle ribbing as she did stand out from the average participant at the ladies mornings. She was younger, more athletic and was naturally attractive without the need for make up which the other ladies wore in thick layers. She was also intelligent and had a part-time job servicing computers for clients of a local firm. One day she made a visit to a client which would change her tennis mornings for ever.

Alison arrived at Jeff Ghandi's house, unaware that he was the Head Coach at the nearby Long Shott Tennis Club and only half registering the tennis trophies as she was led to the computer.

"What seems to be the problem?" she asked cheerfully, as she sat down in his office. "Well, I've had the computer for five years now without any problems. Then last month I read that, after such a long time, computers tend to develop faults which can now be cured by new 'First Aid' software packages. It seemed like a good idea so last week I bought one. I loaded it in this morning and...... the computer crashed!"

Alison laughed and was still chuckling to herself as she began to work on it. In three minutes she had it working again. She didn't fancy returning to the office so quickly, so she offered to show Jeff how to rearrange his document files which were clearly in a mess. She soon discovered that most of the documents were tennis reports and that Jeff was, in fact, Long Shott's Head Tennis Coach. An hour later, after much tennis talk, all the documents were organised.

Jeff was so grateful for the computer tutoring that he offered to give her a free tennis lesson in return. At first she wasn't sure.

She had once talked to a coach in a bar about her forehand and he had suggested she should try co-ordinating the interplay of spatial, temporal and dynamic parameters of motion to enhance her co-efficiency of restitution. This had obviously put her off coaches and lessons. So, by way of a test, she asked Jeff what that meant.

"Move your backside and don't fall over." Came the reply.

This reply, plus the un-high-tech way in which he used his computer, convinced her that she had nothing to fear; the lesson was arranged for the following week.

The lesson went well. She was bright and learnt very quickly. By the end of the session Alison had made considerable progress with her forehand and backhand and was keen to put them into practice at the club ladies mornings. She thanked Jeff very much and arranged for another lesson the following week. One thing, however, greatly disturbed her.

The theories and explanations that had just improved her game so much, bore no relation whatsoever to the tried and tested methods worked out by the ladies at the club. For example, it now appeared that the ball didn't have to skim the net on every shot, you didn't have to hold the racket in a death grip and, worst of all, from time to time you were allowed to enter "no man's land" in the centre of the court. How could she possibly break the news to her friends? This would be going against established, agreed and accepted methods of practice which had been built up over years of coffee.

She decided she couldn't cause unnecessary upset to her friends and instead kept quiet about what she now knew. Over the next few weeks she continued to improve quickly in the lessons; twice a week she also continued to say "good shot" every time the ball skimmed the net and looked suitably apologetic when her partner berated her for entering "no man's land."

However, it became increasingly difficult to hide how quickly she was improving and when pushed one night, she confided in her best friend from the club, Katrina. She told her that she had been having lessons and that what she was learning was too different to what was accepted at the club to be able to mention it. She felt much better.

However, Katrina found it more difficult to keep this news quiet. Before long, all the ladies at the club knew why Alison was improving so quickly, although Katrina made them promise not to let Alison know they knew. In return for this, Katrina promised to find out what the key tips were that Alison was given and pass them on. This pact had an astonishing effect on the overall standard on the tennis at the ladies mornings. It plummeted. The ladies got worse and worse as the Chinese whispers became less and less accurate.

Jeff would tell Alison how to use her forehand semi-western grip to get topspin and, within four days, the Middleside Tennis Club ladies were whispering to each other that, as you hit your forehand, you should spin like a country and western dancer. He told her to use her backhand topspin more and word reached the ladies that to get topspin you should use your back more than your hand.

Things hit an all time low at the club four days after Jeff had taught Alison to throw the ball up over her shoulder for the American twist serve. There were more double faults served that day than ever before, except from those who had heard that Alison had thrown up over her shoulder after one American bourbon twist too many.

The tennis was suffering badly. The techniques, which had been less than smooth before, now instigated the heaviest sales of elbow braces the local sports shop had ever known; extra high fences had to be erected next to the local gardens and all four teams began to slip inexorably down the Spin Valley League tables.

Not only was the tennis suffering but so was Jeff's reputation. Alison would tell Katrina that Jeff had a good backhand and she had taken to the idea of playing drop shots. Word got round that he took backhanders and dropped his shorts.

Alison quietly observed the chaos at the ladies morning. Unaware of her influence, she put it down to the new filter coffee the club had recently switched to. Katrina, however, knew exactly what was happening and was beginning to lose sleep worrying about it.

There was only one answer. A coach had to be employed for one hour a week to put things right. She put the suggestion to the committee and they agreed.

Fortunately for the ladies, they employed one of the worst coaches in all Spin Valley. He told them to aim to skim the net with every shot, grip the racket as tight as possible and under no circumstances enter "no man's land." It was the most effective coaching ever given and soon the standard was restored to what it was before. The teams began to climb up the leagues again, elbow braces were discarded and the fence extensions were taken down.

The only player not attending the club coaching sessions was Alison. She continued with the other club sessions and with Jeff and later that year was a popular winner of the Ladies Club Singles title. No one minded losing to her, even if she was different. She was always generous enough to say "good shot" if the ball skimmed the net.

# SPIN VALLEY INTERNATIONAL

*What is an international tennis player? Is the game the same the world over? Do coaches coach differently from one country to another? Do different tennis teams prepare to compete differently? Can you spot in junior competitions and matches players destined for the heights of the game? Cap Problema. No problem. The strange events that unfold here begin to suggest answers to these niggling questions.*

"Where are the Spanish team? Have you seen them yet?" asked Jeff Gandhi.

Mitch shook his head, "No sign as yet" he said

It was the day before the Spin Valley International Junior Team Challenge. The three-day event, which involved eight international teams, was being held on the hard courts of Long Shott Tennis Club for the first time and the organisers, headed by Senior Club Coach Jeff Ghandi, were keen for it to be a successful one.

Long Shott's popular Club Captain Mitch had been drafted in as a volunteer, a last-minute replacement for Boris Munster who retracted from volunteering activities due to a sore finger. This was one of many injuries Boris Munster claimed throughout the course of a season - all of which seemed to appear when some kind of commitment was required - leading Mitch to call all of his injuries 'head injuries'.

Mitch had stepped in to help out, but in truth he didn't want to be behind a help desk at the tournament for the next three days because he had his own tennis to focus on. He had reached the final of the Long Shott Tennis Club Veterans Open Championships and was due to play on the evening of this tournament's final day. The two events had been planned to coincide so there would be a bigger crowd for the evening barbeque. His game was a little rusty and he needed to practice, not sit behind a desk.

However, he was designated as the official point of contact for the foreign team captains, had the grand title of 'International Liaison Officer' and was now sat in the tournament office getting used to his new role. The office was in fact a Portakabin with two rooms. One in which all enquiries regarding the tournament were received, and one private office for the referee Oliver Mottershed. Mottershed was an officiously efficient man who was not aware of any grey areas between black and white and who was not to be disturbed "unless urgent." The front office therefore contained two tables pushed together where Mitch squeezed in alongside Jeff Gandhi who was responsible for the overall organisation of the tournament.

All the international teams had arrived throughout the day except for the Spanish who were characteristically late. By comparison, the Austrians had arrived exactly on time and by now, appeared to know more about the tournament regulations than the tournament committee. The Austrian captain, Hans, came into the office.

"We would like to practice now," he said. "It is precisely 90 minutes since we ate and we would like to practice now."

"Fine," said Mitch with a smile, "I think court seven is available."

"We prefer to practice on the same court where we will play tomorrow" he said. Mitch looked uncertain and replied "I'm not sure about that - all the courts are the same surface and court seven is free at the moment."

"No, I'm sorry. We like to pay good attention to detail. There may be important differences in the details of the court, such as the balance of light and shade from the trees at the side of the court, the type of surface, speed of the surface, and other environmental surroundings. Please find out which court we will play on tomorrow," said the Austrian captain.

Mitch looked at him patiently and reflected on the excellent courts available, compared with the Whitehaven hospital court on which he often practiced. He wondered if the tufts of grass, broken glass and gritty areas would count as differences in surface speed or simply difference of surface. He wondered if the tree roots growing up through the baseline would be considered 'environmental factors'.

He turned to go into the referee's office to ask about the courts. Before Mitch could ask the question, Oliver Mottershed replied "Court five."

"Thank you," said Mitch as he returned to his office.

"The plan is that tomorrow you will play on court five, so if you would like, court five will be available for practice in one hour, ok?"

Hans looked perplexed. "This is not good news, this practice time would take my players beyond the optimal time when the carbohydrates from our food will transfer to glycogen in the bloodstream. However, we will manage and we will trust you that there are no significant differences between court five and court seven. So we will practice now as this will allow us to stretch dynamically, practice, stretch statically, eat, relax and sleep according to our planned schedule for the evening."

Mitch thanked him although he was not sure why. Hans stood still - he appeared to be waiting. After a moment, he said "We expect you to provide us with practice balls. They should be new balls which are of course all the same brand and at the same temperature as the balls that we will be using tomorrow in the tournament."

"Well," said Mitch, "I am pleased to say I have a spare can of balls for you and as it happens they are of the same brand that will be used in the tournament." And with a twinkle in his eye, he added "But I believe it will be a sunnier day tomorrow and it could be approximately 2° hotter according to our somewhat inaccurate British weather forecast but unless you are going to pop them in the kitchen oven for five minutes I don't think there's much we can do about the temperature!"

"Thank you," said Hans and he left the office with his team of players. Mitch noticed that Hans sent the players to the court to warm up whilst he turned with the can of balls in his hand and headed off towards the cafeteria.

"What time did the Spanish team land at Heathrow?" asked Mitch.

"Over nine hours ago," said Jeff, "We sent Arkwright in the town council's minibus to meet them and they should have been here over two hours ago."

At that moment the telephone rang in the tournament office and Jeff answered… "Ah, Arkwright…oh dear…fan belt…M25…waited two hours for recovery?…Oh dear…see you when you get here." He hung up and turned to Mitch:

"They're on their way. By the way, thanks for helping out this weekend Mitch, it's much appreciated."

"No problem though I must admit that with the Vets Club Open Champs coming up, I was hoping to get some practice in over the next couple of days. I need to work on my first serve and my forehand, neither of which are doing much damage at the moment."

"I can give you a hit tomorrow for an hour once we have all the matches on court, if there's a spare indoor court and I'm sure there'll be others here who will be keen to practice."

"Thanks," said Mitch "But I've been chatting to the foreign coaches as they arrived and a few of them said they would be happy to practice to get some exercise for themselves and a couple have even offered to give me some coaching tips!" Mitch thought this sounded interesting. He was a natural player who won matches through variety, touch and feel. He had never really had any formal 'coaching.'

"The Russian coach said he was available at 6 pm, so I'll go and look for him then."

At 6.40 pm, Mitch was gasping for air. He had never played for 40 minutes continuously without a break in his entire life. The Russian coach, Vladimir, had a hopper full of tennis balls and fed one after the other, shouting at Mitch "You hit! You run! Run harder!" after every ball. Mitch had tried to pause for breath but Vladimir refused to let him stop, shouting aggressively "You hit!" every time Mitch put his hand up.

Jeff saved the day via the loudspeaker:

"Would the International Liaison Officer please make his way to the tournament office." Mitch thanked Vladimir and explained that he had now to do his job for the tournament. Vladimir shrugged his shoulders and went off to find the gym. Mitch staggered in the direction of the office, passing the car park where a huge AA recovery lorry rolled in with a minibus perched on top containing the Spanish team. They climbed out of the minibus and jumped off the back of the truck. Far from being stressed they were singing at the top of their voices.

The Spanish coach introduced himself:

"Hola, I am Carlos. Tell me something!"

"Pleased to meet you, I'm Mitch, I'll be looking after you while you're here. Anything you need - just let me know. Glad you're here - it's been a long journey for you. How long has it taken in total to travel from Spain?"

"Long journey but no problem - Cap problema! Let me see. It has taken…." He broke off and paused while he worked out what he wanted to say, then the phrase he thought he was looking for dawned on him as he loudly announced "How many times have you?"

"Pardon?!" said Mitch.

"How many times have you?" said Carlos.

Mitch was speechless.

"On your time machine?" said Carlos pointing to Mitch's watch.

"Oh… 6.45," he said.

"Then it has taken many times!" said Carlos.

Mitch laughed. He was happy to see Carlos. He didn't like to lose foreign teams, but more importantly Carlos had provided the opportunity to escape the Vladimir cardio session.

"You must be very hungry – let me take you to the restaurant," said Mitch

"No, no we want practice. We eat late in Spain. Tell me, could you give practice balls and a court?"

Remembering his earlier experience, he asked Carlos if he would like to play on the same court as they would play on tomorrow. Looking shocked, Carlos said "No! Why?"

Mitch just smiled and asked if he would like to play with the official brand of tournament balls.

"Tell me." said Carlos "In this tournament, do you play with the round, yellow balls?"

"Yes." said Mitch.

"Well give me some of those!" replied Carlos.

The Spanish team practised for two hours until it was almost dark then left to look for a restaurant in town, singing Spanish songs as they went.

### *Spin Valley International Junior Team Challenge - Day 1*
The format included a separate boys and girls event with two singles matches and a deciding doubles match if the score in the tie was one match all. Round robin groups of four teams played each other on the first two days, resulting in two teams qualifying for the semi-finals to be played out on the final day.

The tournament had progressed well on day one. The weather had been good and all the players seemed to be happy. The fantastic level of play together with the different approaches of the international teams created a buzz around the tournament, but Mitch's mind was constantly on his match on finals day, particularly his forehand, which in his current form, seemed to be 'missing in action'. With this in mind, at the start of day two, Mitch had asked the Austrian coach Hans if he would give him some specific coaching on his forehand. Hans had agreed provided Mitch guaranteed that he eat a banana before beginning the lesson, as scheduling a session over lunch was 'not really sensible'.

The 30 minute practice went reasonably well as Mitch did in fact get to hit a lot of balls at the correct pace and time as opposed to the Russian onslaught the day before. Mitch appreciated the long explanations of how best to use 'elastic energy', 'the angle of separation', 'eccentric muscle contractions' and the role of internal rotation on the cross court-dipping-forehand-passing shot. Not because he could understand them but because they gave him time to get his breath back.

### Spin Valley International Junior Team Challenge - Day 2
The next morning Carlos rolled into the office with his players, his broad smile and an exuberance of Spanish charm, answering every question with "Cap problema."

"Carlos, why do you always say 'Cap Problema?' What does it mean?" asked Mitch.

Carlos gave his usual broad smile and said "It means 'No problem' it is our Catalan approach, our philosophy of life…relax, no problem, don't worry."

"Thanks," said Mitch "your practice court is court 13."

"Cap problema." smiled Carlos as he walked away.

The tournament began to become more meaningful as matches progressed towards the semi-finals and by mid-afternoon, four teams in the boys and girls events, including the Austrians, could no longer qualify for the semi-finals. Hans was philosophical about this; his boys had, in fact, performed particularly well but had eventually been beaten by the stronger Spanish team. Nonetheless he was soon to be seen in the cafe conducting a thorough review of the team's pre-match preparation.

Mitch wondered about this result. As far as he could see, the Austrian team were the most professional, best rested, well prepared team in the tournament. By comparison, the Spanish team had a relaxed approach to pre-match preparation, hadn't eaten until 11 p.m. each night, and didn't see the need for rest when they could be laughing or playing tennis (usually both), which only left about 7 hours sleep a night. He asked Carlos why the Austrain preparation hadn't paid off.

Carlos replied "Easy. Tennis is not about following an expected plan, it is about expecting the unexpected! You have to be ready to solve problems. We are always ready for this! We keep the best attitude for it!"

Later that evening, Mitch managed to get another thirty minutes practice, this time with Jean-Yannick, the French Coach. Jean-Yannick took Mitch through a variety of basket drills which focussed on hitting cross court angles followed by down the line winners. Mitch enjoyed the session and felt like his game was improving. He had rarely worked on the basics. In truth, he had been blissfully unaware of these basics. His basics usually involved dropshots, lobs and wrong-footing reverse spin chips.

*Spin Valley International Junior Team Challenge - Day 3. Finals day*
The semi-finals of both the Boys and Girls events were scheduled for the morning of finals day. The weather was good and the matches began on time to a modest crowd of spectators.

The Spanish continued to dominate the Boys' event in the semi-finals, beating the Swedish team. The Swedes competed well but looked a little weighed down by the expectation that they should all be automatically following in the footsteps of such tennis greats as Borg, Wilander and Edberg.

The French joined them in the final with a somewhat subdued win against the British team, whose top player had to pull out due to injury early in the match.

In the Girls' event, success for the home team of GB against the Belgians was well received and they were now to face the US team in the final, fresh from their surprisingly comfortable victory over the Spanish girls team.

The finals went on court at 1.30 p.m. as planned, the sun was shining and a sizeable crowd had now gathered. The Boys' final began well for France with their number two player, Jean-Luc playing at the top of his game and winning the first set 6-4. Things continued to go well in the second set as he found his way to match point at 6-4, 5-4, 40-30. He then played a near perfect rally and had the Spaniard at his mercy after an excellent approach shot resulting in a poor lob. Jean-Luc decided to end it in style and went for a wrong-footed slam-dunk smash, only to see his shot catch the top of the net and land back on his side of the court as his opponent ran the opposite way from where the ball would have gone had the top of the net not interrupted its path.

This turned out to be a major turning point. For the next ten minutes the French player's head was full of what had just happened so he remained disconnected from the game unfolding on the court in front of him. His resulting 'bad patch' inevitably now coincided with a renewed belief from the Spanish player who saw his opportunity (boosted by the body language of his opponent, the excited encouragement of his Spanish team-mates and a strong awareness of the scoring system). The tennis scoring system is devilish: a system in which a player (in this case Jean-Luc) could be in the lead and seemingly on the way to winning for about 90 minutes, then play poorly for ten minutes and find himself at one set all with the momentum heavily against him. In the final set, Jean-Luc appeared to be playing himself, his opponent and the scoring system. Two of these three was difficult enough but all three resulted in a 6-0 final set in favour of the increasingly excited (if that were possible) Spaniards.

Unfortunately for the French team, their number one was not really in a state to compete effectively in the now critical second match. He had become heavily involved as an increasingly desperate supporter and going onto court to play his match with the team at 0-1 down in the tie, he was emotionally drained. He lost in what can only be described as routine fashion, scarcely filling the role of supporting actor.

The Spanish had won the tie. They had beaten the French, or perhaps more accurately, they were strong and worthy opponents of the French, while the French beat themselves. Nonetheless, Carlos and the Spanish celebrated by, well… being themselves. In truth they had acted like they were celebrating something for most of the tournament so it wasn't tremendously easy to tell, except for the fact they were carrying a trophy around with them.

The Girls' final involved the young American teenage sensation, Destini Dream. She was the youngest girl in the tournament but still good enough to play at number two singles for the US.

She began the match in top gear but was more than matched by the British player, Anne, who was clearly playing well above her normal level. As the match developed, Destini was beginning to get a little frustrated by a series of one-off winners that Anne kept pulling out of the bag on crucial game points. Her frustration continued to build and when Destini netted a volley to lose her serve at 4 games all in the first set, a local fury came across her face and she yelled at the top of her voice "Stop losing!" With the ball she had just missed lying close by at the bottom of the net, Destini took an almighty swing at it with her foot… unfortunately she missed. In itself, this would have been embarrassing enough but having misjudged the kick, her foot followed through and became stuck in the net at about hip height. The immediate outburst of laughter from the crowd did little to quell Destini's anger. Hopping around and becoming increasingly tangled, her face began to mirror the red of her knickers, which were now in full-view of the sniggering spectators.

Referee Oliver Mottershed, who had been watching from close by, now approached the court. He had seen not only that Destini was wearing red knickers but that there was a large Nike swoosh on them. He came onto court stooping, trying to get a proper glimpse of the advertising logo on Destini's underwear.

Destini stared at him and said "What the hell are you doing?"

Mitch's friend and doubles partner Rocket, who was also watching, at that point turned to Mitch and said quietly "He's just checking her backside for ticks."

Mottershed attempted to say with authority: "You do realise that the maximum advertising logo allowed on any item of clothing is 2 inches, don't you? And this also applies to your knickers; knickers, which I may add, should be predominantly white so you are in fact breaking two regulations with one pair of knickers!"

Destini glared at him and said "I would hate to think that I was wearing double regulation breaking knickers, let me take them off!" The referee quickly replied "I don't think that will be necessary. But in future please take care to choose your underwear more carefully." Destini kept her knickers but lost her composure and it was not until 6-4, 5-1 down that she started to play well. At this stage, her opponent's lucky streak appeared to have come to an end and combined with the nerves her opponent was now feeling as a possible end approached, Destini felt the tide was beginning to turn her way. By 4-5, she felt she was actually only a game away from winning the match as Anne was beginning to crumble: her fluidity had gone and she was desperately scrambling and retrieving, hoping for errors from the American. Unless Anne could stumble over this first possible finish line, it would be gone and the final set would be routine.

At 5-4 with the score now standing at deuce, Anne was serving, feeling nervous and looking nervous. She hit her first serve straight into the bottom of the net. She threw the ball up for her second serve, then let it fall without hitting it as a very shakey, mis-placed placement. At the other end, Destini moved around and threateningly tried to put her off. Anne threw the ball in the air and accelerating her racket towards it, struck it with the very top of the frame, sending the ball high over the net, high over Destini's head, and high beyond the fence, travelling towards the clubhouse. Destini screamed "Come on. Right here. Right now!" and changed sides thinking about the breakpoint that was coming up. She appeared to have a boost of energy, fuelled by this unexpected but welcome error from her opponent at this critical stage.

Her coach however had not noticed the change in Destini's body language because she was still tracking the flight of the ball which, having been struck on its under side with the top of the racket, was now spinning backwards. It continued to rise until it ran out of speed above the clubhouse where it hung suspended, still spinning backwards. At this point it would normally have fallen to earth but a gust of wind caught the ball and in combination with the backspin, reversed its direction back along the flight path on which it had come. Destini's coach let out a small cry of "Destini – look out!" and then watched incredulously as the ball gathered momentum and began to travel back towards the court. Destini looked up, quickly registering the warning, then moved to try to intercept the ball, standing next to the net with her back to her opponent, watching carefully as the ball gathered pace towards the service box. The ball followed a perfect line, backtracking at an angle of 45°, it bounced into the service box. As it passed her, Destini lunged to try to touch it as it flew over the net, back towards her opponent. She failed to make contact and her opponent's supporters leapt to their feet to applaud the most unusual clean ace on a second serve that they had ever witnessed.

Moving from break point up to match point down in the space of a reverse-spin-mis-hit-clubhouse-visiting-wind-assisted-second-serve, would be enough to produce a fiery reaction from even the calmest of players but Destini's was truly spectacular. She turned and threw her racket over the fence as hard as she could. It flew straight up into the higher branches of a tree next to the court and stayed there. Everyone watched in stunned silence as she ran at the fence screaming as she went. Now in a furious state she climbed up the fence, clambered over the top of it and flew at the tree, kicking it until she burst into tears and sat sobbing at the bottom.

When she eventually returned, she took an injury time out to receive treatment on the ankle she had damaged whilst kicking the tree. Oliver Mottershed waited until all this was done and then as she walked back onto court, he defaulted her for a variety of non-knicker related offences.

Being defaulted from the event meant she could no longer compete in any other match and this meant she could no longer compete in the doubles. In turn, this meant as the tie was first to two matches, the tournament was handed to GB by default. Their celebration of the hollow victory was much more subdued than usual, though there was plenty to reflect upon later that evening.

The fact that the match had finished early meant that the crowd had some time to kill before the barbeque in the evening and so after a cup of tea, they wandered over to the main grasscourt where the Long Shott Tennis Club Veterans Open Championships Final was due to begin at 5 p.m.

# MITCH MATCH

Mitch's opponent in the final was known locally as Deagle; a determined player who was renowned for his solid but unadventurous play. One common cause of errors in tennis is making poor decisions about which shot to hit before the ball is struck, often known as poor 'shot selection'. Deagle was the sort of player who had little problems with shot selection as he had very few shots from which to select. He was therefore, the ideal opponent for Mitch: under-equipped to handle Mitch's variety of shot, unable to hurt him and unlikely to pull any rabbits out of the hat if Mitch got him on the run.

Mitch was feeling good. He was free from the tournament office, had had a good week and had got the rustiness out of his system with the variety of practice sessions delivered by international coaches. Furthermore, he had made a conscious decision to enjoy this final. As he walked onto the court, he looked around at the majestic sunlit trees, the hawks soaring high on a warm breeze and the church nestling on the hillside. Why should competing in a tennis match alter the feeling that all was well in the world? He felt relaxed and ready to go.

The first set could not have gone any better and Mitch sat down at the change of ends at 6-1 up. He couldn't have scripted a better set. However, it is a rare match that starts at 'good' progresses to 'very good' and finishes 'great, game over'. The first turning point happened at the start of the second set. It was nothing to do with Deagle's play, it was the fact that the Austrian Coach, Hans, came to sit down to watch. Mitch spotted him in the crowd as he walked out onto court for the second set and immediately wondered if he should have had a banana at the end of the first set. Still slightly distracted by this thought, he missed two forehand returns to go 30-0 down in the first game. Glancing at Hans' worried expression, he spent the next ten minutes trying to work out if he was misjudging the angle of separation between his hips and his shoulders by a few degrees and then sat down at 0-3. He got a banana out of his bag.

He sat down again at 1-4 and glanced up to see that Vladimir, the Russian coach was now sitting next to Hans. Mitch hurried back out onto court and began to play at a much quicker tempo. With the relaxed feeling of the first set now a distant memory, he was partly rushing because he wanted to get back in the lead, partly because he was now feeling nervous, but mainly rushing because he thought that Vladimir looked unimpressed with his work rate. This didn't help and he not only lost the second set 2-6 but quickly went 0-1 down in the third set.

At this point, two things happened. Firstly, as Mitch walked to serve at 0-1, there was only one ball at his end so he turned and shouted over the net: "Pass the ball Deagle." Deagle was a man with very little hair and so wore a wig and wondered if Mitch had meant this deliberately. He stared back at Mitch. The umpire, assuming he hadn't heard, repeated loudly in his direction "Ball Deagle." Staring at the umpire, he struck a ball firmly down to Mitch at the other end.

At the same time, Carlos walked past the back of the court and said:

"Hola Mitch, what is score?"

"One set all," replied Mitch.

"Cap problema," said Carlos.

Mitch immediately felt better. His first serve, which appeared to have deserted him, now returned and with Deagle still unhappy about his exchange of words, Mitch broke serve to go 2-1 up.

At the changeover, Mitch remembered Carlos' further advice to 'solve problems'. Looking up he saw the French coach, Jean-Yannick and decided that by sticking to the basics he would perhaps make things less complicated for himself. It is a strange and interesting fact that at beginner level, the best advice is to move your feet, make good contact and aim to get the ball over the net and into the court. Advice seems to get more complex as you improve until you become good enough to compete in tight situations in finals when the advice again boils down to move your feet, make good contact and get the ball over the net and into court. Mitch focussed on exactly that.

Momentum swung back Mitch's way and the feeling of relaxed control began to return to such an extent that at 5-1 up, it was hard for Mitch to recognise any of the feelings of the second set. On match point, he served and volleyed with the feeling that he now didn't want the match to finish; he played crisply into the forehand corner and had Deagle running from side to side with a series of volleys until he finished off the match with an exquisite backhand that faded away and died to a virtual roll. In a last attempt to retrieve a hopeless situation Deagle lost his balance, went into a semi-dive and skidded along the court on his front.

The crowd clapped with great appreciation and Mitch's doubles partner, Rocket announced rather too loudly "Ha! Spread-Deagled!"

Mitch shook hands with Deagle and heaved a sigh of relief. He looked up at the hillside and felt he had fully regained the perspective he lost for the duration of the second set. The award ceremony took place on court and after receiving his trophy, he gave a speech in which he thanked everyone including the tournament organisers, declaring that the organisation had been 'spot-on', the sponsors' sponsorship had been 'spot-on' and his fellow competitors had delivered play that was 'spot-on'. Finally he wanted to thank the club who had given permission to use the courts but his word-selection was almost as limited as Deagle's shot selection and so he paused after saying "whose support has been…" shaking his head while he looked for a different adjective. But realising he had no other word available at that point, he began to nod his head as the crowd spoke with one voice to finish his sentence for him with… "spot-on."

As he came off court Mitch was joined by Carlos and his doubles partner, Rocket.

"Well done mate. What happened in the middle there? You seemed to be rushing," said Rocket.

Mitch smiled and said "Yes, you could say part of the problem was Russian."

Carlos laughed, slapped him on the back and said:

 "Well played. Spot on!"

"Cap problema." said Mitch.

# IT'S GOOD TO TALK

THE LIGHTER SIDE OF TENNIS

*Talking doesn't always mean communicating as Jeff Ghandi, Head Coach, finds out during a telephone call to an anxious "tennis parent."*

It is late one evening and Jeff Ghandi, Head Coach at Long Shott Tennis Club, phones Mrs Tiffin, mother of James Tiffin. James is one of the players whom Jeff coaches.

Jeff:      Hi. Jeff here.  Just thought I'd ring to see how James got on today?

Mrs T:   He played really well...

Jeff:      Oh did he?

Mrs T:   But...

Jeff:      Yes.

Mrs T:   You know...You know all that work you've been doing on his backhand…

Jeff:      Yes.

Mrs T:   His backhand was terrific.

Jeff:      Good.

Mrs T:   But he kept hitting his forehand long. He's a bit confused about all this grip business you've been

talking to him about and his timing just seemed to go.
I think we should work on his forehand.

Jeff:     Right.

Mrs T:    Of course the wind didn't help.

Jeff:     How did it finish then against Jackson?

Mrs T:    Lost. 6-1, 6-1.

Jeff:     OK. At least it sounds like he worked hard at what
          we've been doing in practice.

Mrs T:    It was a close 6-1, 6-1 though. Nearly all the games
          went to deuce. And he'd have won two more games if
          it hadn't been for some very dodgy line calls.

Jeff:     Would he?

Mrs T:    James had to keep calling the umpire on but all he did
          was to keep making them play the points again.

Jeff:     And he lost them.

Mrs T:    Well... I suppose so, yes.

Jeff:     Who's he playing tomorrow?

Mrs T:    And I think the cold he's got affected his breathing. He

needs to time his grunt but that cold just had him
coughing at all the wrong times.

Jeff: It'll clear up soon, I'm sure.

Mrs T: The first match he played really well by the way.
Against Lawrie.

Jeff: Score?

Mrs T: Lost 6-2, 6-4. He nearly got to a tie break in the
second set.

Jeff: At 6-4 down?

Mrs T: He's two ratings higher, you know, is Lawrie.

Jeff: But don't forget Lawrie's from Spin Valley too. Our
standards are lower due to the lack of competition.
We've talked all this through. He really needs to beat
players from other areas of the country. Like Morgan,
for example.

Mrs T: James got two more games off Lawrie than
Morgan did.

Jeff: That's good.

Mrs T: And it was an awful draw getting Lawrie first off. But
James always seems to get the very worst of draws. He

either gets a top seed and loses or he gets a lower ranked player who he's expected to beat and gets nervous; or he gets a similar-ranked player who he has to beat to get his ranking up and feels the pressure.

Jeff:     Well what would be a good draw then?

Mrs T:   We just never seem to get any luck. Morgan got to play a qualifier in the first round.

Jeff:     Who's he playing tomorrow?

Mrs T:   Not sure.

Jeff:     It's a Round Robin, isn't it?

Mrs T:   Yes.

Jeff:     Then he's playing Morgan isn't he?

Mrs T:   Oh no....

Jeff:     Hello?

Mrs T:   ....

Jeff:     Are you still there?... Barbara?

Mrs T:   Yes. I just spilt the tea I was drinking.

Jeff:     Anyway, I'll call tomorrow. I'm only sorry I can't get
          along to watch. It'll be interesting to see how he gets on.

Mrs T:    Trouble is James gets a bit put off by Morgan's
          sponsorship deals. Morgan's got those high-torsion
          shoes. Much better on clay.

Jeff:     They won't be playing on the clay tomorrow.

Mrs T:    No?

Jeff:     It's forecast really heavy rain. They'll play on carpet.

Mrs T:    But it's a clay court tournament. It says so on the
          programme.

Jeff:     Yes, but it is May and it is Britain.

Mrs T:    So all that coaching you gave him on sliding is no good?

Jeff:     Well not on carpet, normally. But Morgan won't have
          an advantage with the shoes.

Mrs T:    James gets put off by his racket bag too.

Jeff:     Anyway, tell James from me: be positive, play the ball
          not the sponsor and accept the challenge. It would be
          a good one to win.

Mrs T:    Thanks very much for calling.

Jeff:     Bye.

Mrs T:    Bye.

The following day...

Jeff:     Hi. Jeff here. Just thought I'd call to see how James got
          on today?

Mrs T:    He played really well but...you know he got more
          games off Lawrie than Morgan the day before...

Jeff:     Score against Morgan?

Mrs T:    6-1,6-1. But...

End

# RACKET ROCKET SCIENCE

I've designed a brand new racket,
It's simply called 'The Force'.
It's a carbo-techno-Jedi bat,
Of the sci-fi, hi-fly sort.

It's Racket Rocket Science
With a fuel injected mould,
Makes Newton's laws look obsolete
And Astrophysics old.

I've honed the racket perfectly,
With a thousand late-night tests,
In the operation's think-tank lab,
.......Next door's garden shed.

It's a total tennis concept,
With a 'con' in every part,
At a one-off hyped-up, knock-down price,
It's the United State of Art.

With an electro charged up handle,
And a technique micro-chip,
So you get a small electric shot
If your semi-western slips.

It's got a frame that can't be shattered,
Made of kryptonite and wood,
A trillium carbonic alloy,
Elbow-grease and mud.

With a gravity force-field booster chip,
So your dropshots die a death,
And a super-oxy hyper drive,
In case you're short of breath.

And strings that move on contact,
That impart the strangest spins,
The reverse-spin, chip-chop, sling-shot shot
Is one…..that doesn't go in.

And a small red light that flashes
If you stop being mentally tough
And a match flow indicator,
So you know if you're getting stuffed.

And a laser-guided feedback beam,
With a heat-seek guidance thing,
So if you hit 'em where it really hurts
You get a bell that rings.

So if you want to serve a rocket
Just set the flight path Sir,
Flick the switch from 'stun' to 'kill'
And fire like Captain Kirk.

So may The Force be with you,
And a bit of luck of course,
'Coz sure as heck you'll need 'em both,
With rotten shots like yours!

# Parents Under Surveillance

*Tennis blog by Jeff Ghandi from the Long Shott Tennis Club website:*

This year I attended the National Under 16 Championships in Grantchester. I was there in my capacity as Head Coach and to support our players but I also took the opportunity to engage in a little 'parent-watching'. I have always been fascinated by the behaviour of parents at tennis tournaments; in some respects it is more entertaining than watching the players.

I have reached one main conclusion: that most parents cannot bear to watch at exactly the same time as they cannot bear not to watch. The Grantchester Tennis Centre is ideal for this condition as one of its peculiar advantages is the existence of a wide range of permanent and temporary spectator stands. None are very near the courts where the majority of matches are played. Yet such a lack of proximity is a positive advantage to parents anxious to watch but not to watch.

Such parents both possess the eyesight of the bald-headed eagle and seem oblivious to vertigo as they sit perched amid scaffolding in a row of empty green-plastic seats, gazing into the distance and animatedly debating line calls. Their decoding of the score from the blurred outlines of their offspring's body language and from the echoing pitch of grunts and squeals is nothing short of ingenious.

As two parents told me, they have become very experienced at working out the score in this way. It is, they say, a bit easier in the winter when they can watch from behind court-dividing curtains, through toilet windows and from acute angles on balconies. The same parents told me that many tennis parents believe that their presence courtside is inhibiting to their son or daughter's play.

Fathers are particularly interesting to watch as many of them seem to have become seriously amateur coaches to their children. Some even reverse their peaked caps or wear sport wrap-around sunglasses. One father new to tennis had a white bandana (or was it a handkerchief?) tied round his head for the duration of the tournament. Most of them keep showing anyone who will watch them what the shot, complete with grunt, should have been. Mothers usually stand a little apart, watching the fathers rehearse a whole repertoire of mis-shapen backhands and curious stabbing actions only remotely resembling volleys.

Some parents were separated for the duration of their child's match, the tension driving them to watch other matches. However, they managed to keep in contact with each other and with the score through elaborate codes and signalling systems which would put race-course tic-tac men to shame and would have been the envy of Samuel Morse himself!

Some parents do however, prefer a close-up view of things. I call them the 'close-up' parents. They normally lean with well-practised nonchalance against the wire-mesh of the court and seem only vaguely interested in the outcome of the match. They chat casually with other spectators, put their collapsible chairs up and down several times, read newspapers, rearrange extensive banana supplies, finish off the Pro-Tennis game app left uncompleted by their child's call to play or log all the previous day's results into an *iPad*.

For most of the close-up parents the temptation to intervene in line calls, score disputes or tactical ploys is resisted. But for some anything except temptation can be resisted and inevitably, they get involved in on-court disputes. I noted that players with long-standing rivalries nearly always have parents with long-standing rivalries. One particularly tense boys' doubles match late one evening led to considerable verbal abuse and not a little bad language. Thankfully, the players on court managed to exercise greater control.

We all know the truly British parents, however. They exhibit a clenched-teeth courtesy to opposing parents, politely commenting on the length of the journey to Grantchester, the comfort of the local hostelry, the imminent rain... anything except the match itself. Some have developed a disarming way of finding out about the coaching available and I was even asked direct questions about our players by some parents. They reveal little about their own child's coaching though, because they are too busy telling the parents of the child they are playing about the whole hospital-waiting-list of injuries and ailments their child has, which prevents 'us' from reaching our full potential this week. These parents always seem to include themselves with the child, using phrases such as "we won" and "we lost" or "we're not on form at the moment" or "we're suffering a shoulder strain."

Finally, I noticed how many of the watching parents at this year's Nationals were good at watching out for national coaches whom they hoped to influence. Walks were timed to perfection so they arrived courtside at the same time as their targeted prey. The coaches wearing the national sponsor's tracksuit were particularly in demand and were physically jolted in lunch queues so that introductions could be effected. One national coach was even presented with a parent's business card as he entered a Portaloo!

I noticed how many of the national coaches are fast learning a whole range of avoidance strategies. They, too, seem to have developed eagle-eyed vision, recognising at some distance the parents who persist in pointing out the scorching backhand their daughter played just after they had left court side or who require ceaseless explanations of why their child is not yet a nationally-supported player.

Many coaches seem to take refuge in the almost blacked-out, wrap-around sunglasses but I did observe that several coaches, whose deftness of movement may be slightly in decline on court, have now learned, off-court, to execute manoeuvres with a grace and explosive speed that leave all but the most strategic and persistent of parents in their wake.

I could write a novel about the Nationals fortnight but most of you wouldn't have the time to read it. However, I would stress how tennis brings out, like all sports, the best and worst in us. If I've concentrated in this blog on what might appear to be some of the worst aspects of the parents under surveillance then it's because we might need to give more consideration to how tennis involves us all compulsively and that it's not just the players who need coaching. Some of our parents do too.

Jeff Ghandi.

# DEAR MIXED TROUBLES

*Katie Robinson is an experienced national-standard tennis player and coach. For a time she worked at the Long Shott and Spin Valley Clubs as an assistant to Jeff Ghandi, organising group coaching for women's club teams.*

*Katie recently completed a psychology degree and was not sure she wanted to continue coaching in the same way. She spent several months looking into how she might use her qualifications in the world of club and regional tennis. She had thought of becoming more involved with the mental training of the regional junior elite squads or of branching out more widely into sports psychology. But, encouraged by her friends, she decided to set up an on-line 'tennis agony aunt' column for players who want to share the kinds of problems that are specific to tennis. She advertised it as 'A tennis improvement site, offering photographs, videos and on-line guidance for tennis problems such as 'hit that killer second serve' and 'slice your backhand with venom'.*

*The site had a slow start but gradually started to get more hits and to become more popular. At first the problems were those of local club members (most of whom used false names, of course) though she could guess who they might be.*

**Tennis Agony Aunt:**
**Problems with your Tennis?**
**Ask your Tennis Agony Aunt**

*Dear Katie,*

I have been playing with Jack my doubles partner for the last ten years and we have done well in several competitions. He is also a very good friend and I want him to remain a good friend. But he has recently got a lot slower and shows no interest in working on his fitness. He does try to run for balls but it is a bit like starting a barge on a canal. In fact, he plays Cinderella tennis. He never quite gets to the ball.

What should I say to him? Will it affect our friendship? Can you give me some good practice drills for those silky drop volleys the top players play? If Jack can learn this shot, it might mean I can play more at the back of the court and do more of the running. The only problem with this is that of his many talents, talent isn't one of them.

Best wishes,

John Jackspin

*Dear John,*

*This is tricky. In all walks of life talking to your partner about their weight is not recommended. The best plan is to avoid his embarrassment and your frustration by preventing the ball from getting to him as often as possible. To do this, I think you need to intercept more, you know ... it is sometimes called 'poaching'. If it goes well, it would only leave him playing one return of serve or one serve per rally. If it goes very well, you could get away with him playing as little as 18 shots per set.*

*Good luck,*

*Katie*

*Dear Katie,*

Everyone seems interested in spin shots at the club at the moment: backspin, topspin, sidespin, slidespin, slicespin...makes my head spin! Can you explain what spin is please? I don't want to look out of place in discussions with the other players. Can you give me a phrase that can be added to any conversation which makes me seem knowledgeable? I don't have to understand what it means, just one good phrase would be great. On another matter - Is it ok to wear make-up during tennis matches? I look rather lined without it and I want to make sure I look attractive to other club members. Trouble is, when I sweat the eye-liner runs and my face can look a bit like a zebra. Finally, what's the best strategy for playing but not breaking into a sweat?

Thanks,

Gloria Honeybone

*Dear Gloria,*

*Thank you for your email. It has caused me to examine the aims of this column very carefully. The best way I can describe spin is that it makes the ball rotate in one direction or another and this has an effect on the air pressure which, depending on the speed, flight path, wind and surface.........hhmm you're right, just drop this phrase into the conversation: "Did you know that most shots have a range of inbound ball spins between zero and 4000 rpm (400 rad/s)?" Then just smile. That should do it. With regard to your make-up problem, you're right, not sweating on court will solve this and I have the answer. It's simple really - sweat usually involves effort so I would try to develop an effortless style of play.*

*Hope that helps!*

*Yours sincerely,*

*Katie.*

**Katie started the site believing that the letters she received would contain a sample of the most common shot-making problems of club-standard tennis players and was hopeful that she might collect them**

*into a book that really helped improve standards.*
*But Katie's site has now gone not just national but global. She now receives over a hundred postings a week from around the world and only has time to answer three or four each week. Yet, strangely perhaps, most of the problems that people write to her about have little directly to do with tennis!! She decided to change the name of her web-site.*

### Dear Mixed Troubles,

My coach keeps posting videos of my serve but I am unable to access the site, though he has sent me a black and white photo. I keep phoning him but he can only send me links which never seem to work on my PC. He promised the site would be personal and private but the link he creates feeds into *YouTube* and I am worried that other members at my club will see my serve. What should I do? Also my chest looks much larger than I remember it and wonder if the coach might have been using some kind of digital enhancement.
April MacMahon,
Brisbane Australia.

### Dear Mixed Troubles,

I have joined my club with a view to romance and finding a new partner after my recent divorce. But there are no men in my cardio class. The ladies in my class are all really friendly and keep encouraging me to play doubles in the weekly get together. I do but I really want to play mixed doubles. Would it look bad if I wrote to the club committee suggesting many more mixed doubles cardio classes and competitions? And, yes, I am interested in learning how to smash. Can you show me some

videos that also help show off your figure to its best advantage when you smash?
Jill from Nuneaton, UK.

### Dear Mixed Troubles,

I am forty seven years young and am still active as a tennis player, playing in club matches and competitions. I am finding it very difficult to bend down to pick up balls when playing matches. In social doubles matches I brought my dog onto court but he became distracted and started chasing the balls while they were still in play. Can you suggest what I should do? Would it look bad if I brought a ball hopper onto court during matches? Do you have any pictures or videos showing seniors picking up tennis balls without having to bend down? What do you think other players will think of me? I am only forty seven.
Algie from New Jersey, USA.

### Dear Mixed Troubles,

My wife is spending a lot of time at the tennis club. We do not talk to one another like we used to. She has also taken to spending a lot of money on tennis outfits with quite short skirts and shorts. Should I be suspicious? She has never worn shorts in her life before.
Worried of Wyoming, USA.

### Dear Mixed Troubles,

Our club has photos of all the members on a large notice board with the aim of improving 'mutual recognition' and 'bonding' and to help with the identification of players in competitions. The trouble is the photo they have used is the one I sent in with my membership application. It's an old passport photo-booth one I had available at the time and has a dark background that makes me look a bit like a police suspect. I am worried that, looking like this, I won't get many invitations to play in doubles tournaments or the kinds of social doubles tournaments where I might meet new friends. I requested that the club secretary replace my photo and I sent in a new one but she texted me to say that the original photo looked better on the board. What shall I do?

Oh, and by the way, can you direct me to the sections of your web-site about hitting a backhand slice? I am really struggling with this. But I am struggling more with worries about my photo. Jonathan @jon.co.nz

p.s. Do you think it'll look better if I send them an action photo? What about a picture of me hitting a backhand slice 'with venom' as on the home page of your web-site? That'll make me look more masculine, won't it?

### *Dear Mixed Troubles,*

I jus cant git intu our joonya team. It sukz. David Jenkins allwayz makes it. I win alot of matchis agenst David Jenkins in practis but he is allwayz silectid above me. The coach sez he has betta shotts and more long-term potenshull an that its not all about winnin. Why duz the coach lyk him so much? He tellz me I need tu work more on my shott-makin an I am writin tu ask if you can show me sum videos of volleeez or giv me some practis shotts. My coach sez I hav trubul reedin the game. He sez he needs edukated playaz. But onlee last night l beat David Jenkins 6-4, 6-2. Shud I giv up? How do I find a way tu show wot I can do in matchis? Shud I work on my reedin and writin?

Kyle Watson from Luffbra Boyz

*Dear Mixed Troubles,*

Over the past few years I have started to go bald. Can you recommend tennis caps that will help cover things up? Do you think a baseball cap looks out of place? Do you think a cap will go with a new routine for a smash? I am only forty three years of age.

David from Perth, Western Australia.

*Dear Mixed Troubles,*

How can I stop my doubles partner apologising after every shot?
Daniel of Bradenton, Florida.

*Dear Mixed Troubles,*

My mixed doubles partner has obviously been watching too much Wimbledon and wants to high five after every point we win. She also looks at my chest when we do this. I have to have the buttons open on my tennis shirt as I get very hot when playing. Is there a tactful way of stopping this? She always has a glint in her eye. I don't know whether she is being flirty or ultra competitive? It's giving me sleepless nights.

Michael from Newport, Wales.

**Conclusion**: As John McEnroe is supposed to have said: "I don't want to sound paranoid but the electronic line judge knows who I am."

# CALLING THE SHOTS

*Gentle, unassuming and largely incompetent, Cedric Ballsworthy shows hidden qualities. Lurch and Sharkey McFly, a dangerous doubles partnership, are distinctly unimpressed.*

Cedric Ballsworthy was the head umpire in the Spin Valley Umpires Association. He had qualified as an umpire in 1969 and had been umpiring, despite a sizeable degree of incompetence, ever since.

He even umpired at Wimbledon on a regular basis. He was very proud of this fact, even if it was only as a linesman on the far tramline in the 'Over 55s' ladies doubles. In fact, he considered this to be the top job; for, after all, these were the gracious mature ladies of the fairer sex. No-one could argue with this point of view, though it was perhaps fair to say that the ball would not often be travelling at a speed to test his eyesight.

Cedric Ballsworthy was a kindly man, and often showed a trait unusual for umpires when doing their job… humanity. Cedric was much less supercilious and officious than some of his colleagues. He understood that it was possible to be flexible on the dress code and that it wasn't vital to address eight-year-old Jason as "Mr Smith" in a mini tennis line-call dispute.

For these reasons, he was as popular as an umpire can get. "It is nice to see Cedric in the chair," old lady spectators would often say as they waved at him from the bench at the side of the court. "Such a shame he can't make us out from over there."

The day he went to umpire at the Veterans Summer National Cup finals started well. He had spent some time in the umpires' area which, as is usual at tournaments, was cordoned off, away from the players' area so that no friendships could be formed, no on-court disputes continued nor the conversations of the umpires overheard. This was just as well as their conversations are often strange and regularly involve the establishment of a kind of officiating hierarchy, created by elaborate tests on the most obscure of rules, to which they will gleefully subject one another.

As usual, Cedric sat apart from the younger, more ambitious umpires for he had little in common with them. They had qualified as umpires by passing through a rigorous training regime in which they received an encyclopedic education; they even knew from which side you should serve if play were to be interrupted by a mad axe man.

The match of which Cedric was in charge was a crucial one, an unfinished match from the day before. Arkwright Stone and Jeff Ghandi were facing the number one seeds, Lurch and Sharkey McFly, in the semi-final.

Thirty minutes before the match, Cedric had his first chance encounter with the McFly brothers. He was washing his hands in the toilets, when in strolled Lurch and Sharkey. They stood next to him, also washing their hands. Breaking the somewhat awkward silence, Cedric felt the need to assert himself: "Gentlemen, although I have to inform you that I am, in fact, from the same club as your opponents, I assure you that should a situation arise in which I am in any doubt as to the legitimacy of the point, I will call the lines in your favour, to equal things out."

The McFlys stared at him. "Well anyway, have a nice play," he said and turned to leave.

He had been hoping to get out quickly but the first three doors he tried were locked. He tried them all again; still locked. The McFlys stared at him. With more force now he yanked at each of them but none opened. Beginning to panic, he turned and said: "Someone's locked us in, we could miss the match." By this stage the McFlys' eyebrows were raised in a bemused, almost shocked expression. Then Cedric's eyes at last focussed on the exit on the other side of the room as he realised that he had been trying to open the engaged toilet cubicles.

"Ah, anyway, break a leg," he said and left as the McFlys continued to stare in disbelief.

Just before the match was due to start, he met them again at the referee's table. "I'll just go and check the court is ready," said Cedric and went through the door, closing it behind him. Immediately Cedric was surrounded by darkness. He had just shut himself in the storage cupboard. For some considerable time he stayed in the storage cupboard trying to think of a plausible reason for having have done this. No reason came however, and the longer he stayed in, the greater the pressure was to think of a convincing excuse. After a full two minutes he opened the door a crack and peeped out. Inevitably, the McFlys were staring at him.

They eventually went on court and the match began. Cedric was concentrating hard. The match reached 3-3 in the third set.

So far he had got the score wrong twice, fallen out of his chair once and had three calls questioned. The one foot fault he had called had been ignored by Lurch McFly who claimed he simply thought it was a late call from the previous rally.

At 5-5, all four players had had enough and it was agreed that they should call their own lines. Cedric should rule on any disputes and call the score, even though Cedric had already called game, set and match at 5-4 by mistake.

When the players finally focussed on the game, the play was outstanding and the match came to a climax when Stone and Ghandi stood at match point on Lurch's serve at 7-8. Lurch stood ready to serve, looked up for a second and then with the energy of fury from being match-point down, unleashed one of the hardest serves ever seen at the Veterans National Cup. Instead of taking its destined path to become an ace, Jeff Ghandi somehow got his racket on it and it shot back for a clean winner down the line.

His supporters went wild and Cedric heaved a sigh of relief that the match was over. He drew breath to announce game, set and match for the second time, but Lurch and Sharkey failed to come to the net to shake hands. Instead, they took up a position as if to replay the point.

"Foot-fault. Second serve," announced Lurch in the most innocent of voices. Everyone looked at him and a stunned silence descended.

"Listen, we agreed we'd call the linecalls. You call the lines on your side of the net, we call them on ours. I foot-faulted on that serve, and I'm calling it. Second serve." Lurch stood his ground.

Chaos ensued for a brief minute until, unexpectedly, Cedric took control of the situation. With an authority never heard before in his voice he announced:

"Incorrect interpretation of rule 34, paragraph 5, subsection 43 which (and I quote) clearly states:

'In the event of the hitherto aforementioned self-jurisdiction circumstance, the extremity of the leg below the ankle materially affecting the initial location is inconsequential if the player's optical focus is directed at the ball which shall be more than 6.35 cm and less than 6.67 cm in diameter.' Game, set and match."

The McFlys came to the umpire's chair but no words came out. Stunned and speechless they stood staring into space. Cedric climbed down from his chair, shook both their hands and marched triumphantly off the court as cheers from Jeff and Arkwrights' supporters rang in his ears.

Nobody saw the McFlys come in off the court that night.

Later that year, Cedric was honoured at the Spin Valley Annual General Meeting for his services to the game and his infallible interpretation of the rulebook.

# A RUSH OF AIR

I looked at my opponent
As I walked out onto court,
That grin was one I thought I knew,
Perhaps we'd met before.

I glanced up at the score board,
For this crucial club home game,
Milos…Ra…Ra…Raonic,
That's not a local name.

I was fighting fit and eager,
My mind was strong as steel,
I could stroke or punch or sock it,
With power, touch or feel.

I was ready for the challenge,
The battle, the fight, the match.
Prepared, equipped and ready,
Just not for a serve like that.

I didn't see the first few,
Just felt a rush of air,
Knew not what side they past me on,
He scarcely seemed to care.

I stepped up to the line again
Feeling pretty tense,
I saw the ball, but saw it late,
I swung… it hit the fence.

I tried to increase my focus,
Got me self psyched up,
I watched the ball so closely…
Then turned to pick it up.

I stood and left a gap one side,
A cunning plan in mind,
I turned to hit a forehand,
The ball flew past behind.

The next one somehow hit my strings,
With a mighty shuddering clout,
I sprang up for the rally,
But the umpire called it out.

He served another rocket,
This time I was in luck,
'Til it hit a stone in the service box,
I had to twist and duck.

And whilst lying face down on the floor,
I suddenly saw the light:
"I need to get aggressive,
To make him tense and tight."

So I danced a scary dance routine,
My eyes glowed firey red,
I struck a pose and glared at him,
To fill his mind with dread.

I pierced his mind with a show of strength,
He surely felt downcast,
He bounced it once and hit it,
And I watched the ball fly past.

"I've had enough of this," I said,
With the stiffest upper lip,
I stood a little further back,
And took a stronger grip.

I held my ground, my jaw clenched tight,
A grim look on my face,
Like a battle hardened warrior,
I prayed against an ace.

His body coiled as he threw it up,
His arm was poised to whack it,
But as he swung, he missed the ball,
And cracked his leg wi' his racket.

The air was filled with a mighty cry
As he crumpled to the ground,
A cry all filled with terror,
Beyond his grunting sound.

And as the medics carried him off,
I grabbed his hand to shake,
Then turned and told my team mates:
"I knew I'd get a break."

# SPIN VALLEY TENNIS GLOSSARY

L.S. T.C.

LONG SHOTT TENNIS CLUB
*Since 1876*

ENTHUSIASTICUS
DESPITUS
ELEMENTUM

**Baseline** - two octaves below the service line.

**Baseliner** - the groundsman.

**Chip 'n' charge merchant** - club caterers.

**Country and Western grip** - no such thing.

**Fault** - "Boo."

**Deuce** - a pre-requisite of Mitch holding his serve.

**Doublefault** - "Boo-boo."

**Down the line** - rarely attempted by Spin Valley players.

**Drop-shot** - similar to Rocket's lobs.

**Foot-fault** - penalty for kicking your opponent.

**Groundstroke** - bouncing your racket down in anger.

**Half-volley** - when the volleyer attempts a volley but misses it.

**Knock up** - only needed if you sleep in.

**Love** - pointless in tennis.

**Many Happy Returns** - unlikely if facing Rocket's serve.

**No man's land** - the grass courts at Dipton.

**Overheads** - usually costly.

**Semi-western grip** - not the opposite of semi-eastern grip,
which doesn't exist.

**Serve and volley** - doesn't count if punctuated by six groundstrokes.

**Slice backhand** - backhand played with backspin.

**Slice serve** - serve played with no backspin.

**Tie-break** - not to be confused with "tea-break."

**Tramline** -more sensible than the American version "Alley."

**Vets tennis** - not necessarily referring to sick animals.

**Western grip** - not the opposite of an eastern grip.